The Gray Warriors

Carol Lavelle Snow

Howard Thomas Snow, Jr.

iUniverse, Inc.
New York   Bloomington

The Gray Warriors

Copyright © 2008 by Carol Lavelle Snow & Howard Thomas Snow, Jr.

All rights reserved. No part of this book may be used or reproduced by any means, graphic, electronic, or mechanical, including photocopying, recording, taping or by any information storage retrieval system without the written permission of the publisher except in the case of brief quotations embodied in critical articles and reviews.

This is a work of fiction. All of the characters, names, incidents, organizations, and dialogue in this novel are either the products of the author's imagination or are used fictitiously.

iUniverse books may be ordered through booksellers or by contacting:

iUniverse
1663 Liberty Drive
Bloomington, IN 47403
www.iuniverse.com
1-800-Authors (1-800-288-4677)

Because of the dynamic nature of the Internet, any Web addresses or links contained in this book may have changed since publication and may no longer be valid. The views expressed in this work are solely those of the author and do not necessarily reflect the views of the publisher, and the publisher hereby disclaims any responsibility for them.

ISBN: 978-0-595-52327-6 (pbk)
ISBN: 978-0-595-62383-9 (ebk)

Printed in the United States of America

Contents

Prologue: Surprise Attack	1
Part One: The First Surprise Attack	3
Part Two: Dark World Revisited	19
Part Three: Welcome to Lima	39
Part Four: Eradicating Cocaine	63
Part Five: Rescue Mission	87
Part Six: Sendero Rampage	101
Part Seven: Down in Enemy Territory	117
Part Eight: The Battle of Santa Lucia	135
Part Nine: Merry Christmas	175

Prologue: Surprise Attack

The Santa Lucia Base in Peru - 1990

It started as an ordinary Friday night. The Peruvians rebels—the communists or *Sendero Luminoso* as they called themselves and the drug traffickers—sometimes attacked our base on the weekends—if the moon was full—if it was dry. Well, the moon wasn't full. It wouldn't be full for another week. But it wasn't raining. So we figured there might be an attack.

The Peruvians always came from one direction in the valley and positioned themselves across the Huallaga River that ran past our base or on the island in the river. When we saw movement in either area, we knew the enemy was in place.

We would wait, and here they would come—blowing their whistles, banging their horns, and blowing ooga horns to build up their courage, most of them drunk and high. It was a big party to them.

When they got to about 300 meters, we fired off some flares to illuminate the ground so they would know they'd been spotted. They'd shoot their guns three or four times and run back in the direction they'd come from.

These battles were certainly nothing for us to be too concerned about.

So that night we sat around the tent after dinner and watched a video and some of the guys played poker.

I didn't get involved in the games. I was an inspector, in charge of our helicopters, and had paperwork to do. So when Bruce Lee finished kicking the bad guys into shape, I decided I'd better walk down the gravel road to my shop. Without thinking about it, I slipped a 9-millimeter pistol and two extra clips into the belt holster I carried in the back of my shirt and started down the road.

The base was quiet, except for Irish whose complaints about his cards and the laughter of the others followed me out the door. Except for my boots crunching gravel and the muffled sound of music coming from the building where the Peruvian officers stayed.

Searchlights from the two towers far to my right glided along the trees and brush across the river. There was no sign of movement. On the base itself lights illuminated the area around the tents and around the helicopter pads. But my shop, which was an open shed enclosed with wire fencing, sat at the back of the base, half a mile from the tents, close to where the runway ended, its sharp edges softened by moonlight.

The air seemed cooler than usual, not quite as damp, and the stars over the jungle beyond my shop seemed a little brighter.

I went inside, turned on the lights and did the weekly report of how many hours the helicopters had flown then made a list of parts we needed to order. When I'd finished, I put the papers in the filing cabinet and turned off the lights.

Immediately I heard something—whispers, people moving.

I walked out the front and went to the side of the building and stopped and listened before I realized what was going on.

People were moving in front of me, on each side of me, and behind me. They had infiltrated the base.

Instead of coming down the big valley the way the terrorists usually came, some of them had come through the fence behind my shop, but most of them were coming down the runway, which ended 100 yards to my left. They were coming from a new direction—and there were hundreds of them.

Fear washed over me.

I was trapped, half a mile from the other Americans. Surrounded by the enemy. For the second time caught in a surprise attack.

I'd barely survived the first attack. I'd been lucky that time. But it looked like my luck was running out.

Part One:
The First Surprise Attack

Chapter One

An Oil Exploration Camp in the Amazon Basin - 1986

I KNEW IT was a dream. Grandpa was dead. He couldn't be standing in front of me looking so concerned. So I knew I was dreaming. Then he started talking, his words forceful, urgent, but I couldn't quite make out what he was saying. But it was very important, something I needed to know, something I needed to understand.

Then I was aware of a dull pain in my right side and rain stinging my face and woke up with that same sense of urgency I'd felt in the dream. And it came back to me—the attack. I'd been doing a daily inspection of the helicopter, when somebody jerked me off the work deck and stuck a pistol in my face.

I hit him with the only thing I had, a breaker bar ratchet I'd been using to change an igniter plug. I knocked the man down; and the gun went off.

When he jumped up, he had a big knife in his other hand. That's the last thing I could remember.

The rain slacked off, and I opened my eyes to a gray Peruvian sky and the sound of fires popping and cracking. No sounds of people. But the acrid smell of smoke hung in the air.

I was lying on my back on a concrete landing pad beside the Jet Ranger Helicopter I'd been working on. Sandbags enclosed the landing pad on three sides, making it impossible for me to see the camp, to see if the terrorists were still around. My glasses lay within reach, as if someone had jerked them off and tossed them aside. When I reached over and picked them up, the wound in my side objected; and I could feel warm blood spreading across my stomach.

I gasped and stopped and waited until the pain subsided before putting the glasses on. Only my hands were shaking so much that I had trouble finding my face. Which struck me as funny.

With the glasses securely across my nose, I gingerly touched my side. My pants and shorts had been sliced open, and my fingers found the wound. I couldn't really tell how bad it was. It didn't matter though. In the jungle any wound that isn't treated can kill you, and I had no idea how long I'd been unconscious.

The shot he fired must have grazed my head because I found a crease above my left ear. Blood matted my hair and insects buzzed around my head. But what really upset me, what really made me angry was that someone had taken my baseball hat. I'd fastened some gold WWI pilot's wings to the front of that hat. The wings were practically irreplaceable.

When I raised up, it hurt. So I stopped, caught my breath, and propped myself up on one elbow while I squeezed the flesh between my thumb and forefinger. That's supposed to ease the pain. And maybe it did a little.

The rain beat down more heavily for a while before backing off again, and my whole body started shaking. I needed to find some kind of cover. To get out of the rain. But first I had to make sure the terrorists, the *Sendero*, had gone.

It was hard to move though because my side hurt so much, so I sort of scooted up next to the sand bags on my back and carefully raised up far enough to get a fairly good look at the camp.

Only fires or smoke filled the area where our tents had been. No sign of movement. No sign of the *Sendero*. No sign of anyone else who was alive.

After taking a couple of deep breaths, I scooted off the helicopter landing pad on my rear and inched toward a nearby conex.

The conexes were red metal containers—little one-room apartments that contained two cots, a shower, and a little stove. The oil company had them airlifted into the jungle by big Russian helicopters. They also contained first aid kits. If I could make it to a conex, I could take care of my wounds.

Just off the landing pad, not more than 15 feet away, lay the body of one of the native workers, covered with insects. It wasn't swollen though, so I figured I hadn't been unconscious very long because in the jungle bodies start swelling within about eleven hours.

At the center of the clearing, the cook tent still burned, and bodies lay all around it as well. But I saw no signs of movement.

We'd heard rumors and received notices from the embassy that we should be on a very high state of alert because the communists, the *Sendero*, were trying to capture Americans or Europeans and hold them for ransom. I had a little .38 revolver tucked in the back of my belt, under my shirt; but when one of them pulled me off the work deck, the only thing I'd had readily to fight with was the breaker bar. All I'd managed to do was hit that one person with the bar.

Debris lay across the ground, mostly paper. But close to the building I found a piece of a tarp that had come off the awning in front and dragged it with me.

I was really hurting by the time I made it to the conex, hurting too much to get up and open the heavy metal door, so I decided to rest, just for a little bit. I sat against the building and pulled the tarp around me for a little warmth and protection from the rain. That's when I remembered the dream.

Funny that I'd dreamed about my grandfather. I hadn't thought about that tough, old man for a long time. Grandpa had married three times and outlived two of those wives. He was 96 when he died one night after working in the fields all day, and his hair was just beginning to turn gray at the temples.

Grandpa had probably been the strongest male influence on my life—he and some of his sons. My dad had died from a shot of penicillin when I was seven. My mother had to work and couldn't take care of a young boy during the summers, so I spent them with my grandparents on their farm in Texas.

My grandfather believed strongly in the work ethic. He gave me five cows to milk every morning and evening. I learned how to milk cows, churn butter, and collect eggs, but also how to ride a horse.

I was living a small boy's dream—riding horses out across the vast expanse of country on and around my grandfather's farm.

But what had Grandpa been trying to say in the dream? I had the crazy idea that if I could just make out what he was trying to tell him, I'd be all right. So I took a deep breath, pinched the soft flesh between my left thumb and forefinger again, and tried to ignore the pain in my side and concentrate on what Grandpa had been trying to say. It was something I needed to understand.

THEN I WAS a kid again—back at my grandfather's farm.

The old man was setting up targets for me—sticks.

"Michael Branagan uses cans for target practice. They don't break or anything. Couldn't I use cans?"

I knew Grandpa didn't like the mess breaking bottles make, but cans don't make much of a mess. Besides, you can see the bullet holes and you can hear the bullets hit—better than you can hear bullets hitting sticks.

Grandpa took out a handkerchief and wiped sweat from his brow. The Texas sun was hot, the air still.

"They make a mess, Josh. You have to pick them up and throw them away. Besides, it's harder to hit sticks. You practice with sticks, and you're going to be a better shot than Michael Branagan is."

We walked away from the sticks Grandpa had stuck between a couple of logs, and I put my .22 rifle to my shoulder and took aim at the first one in the row.

"Aim small and miss small," Grandpa called to me.

Then the scene changed. I was in the woods alone. A parrot lay on the ground at my feet. At first it seemed to be breathing, but it wasn't. It was dead, its bright red and green wings spread out across the ground, its blood staining the brown soil.

I AWOKE WITH a start, my heart pounding. I'd heard something. A human voice? Or had it been the cry of a bird? I fumbled for the gun, getting it out of the back of my pants and sat very still, holding it, listening. The jungle seemed unusually quiet. Then a parrot called, far off in the trees, a ghostly, almost ethereal sound.

I shook my head, trying to shake out the cobwebs. My mouth was dry. It had stopped raining, but it was getting dark. I needed to get a drink and give myself first aid before I passed out again. So I had to get inside the conex. Taking a deep breath, I rolled over. Then pressing my left hand against my side, I stood on my knees.

The effort took my breath away. I rested my head against the door until my breathing became normal again, then reached up and, pulling the lever down, pushed the heavy door open.

Inside things were in disarray. One cot had been overturned. Books and papers and some clothes lay across the floor.

The opening was about a foot off the ground, so I leaned forward and crawled over the step and into the room. Just inside the door sat a box containing two water bottles. I opened one and drank it down. Then because it hurt too much to crawl on my hands and knees, I turned over again and scooted toward the back wall where the first aid kit hung.

It wasn't there. Someone had torn it off the wall. Panicked, I scanned the debris on the floor and finally saw it by the overturned cot, partially hidden in the shadows of the room. I scooted over and rummaged through it, finding what I needed--packets of sulfur powder. Then I backed up against the wall and, after resting for a couple of minutes, pulled my bloody shirt and pants aside.

A deep gnash about 18 inches long ran down my right side. The incision had slashed my jeans and cut my belt in half, but the belt had probably saved my life. However, if I didn't stop the infection and do it quickly, I'd die.

There was a bottle of alcohol in the kit, but I knew better than to use it. I'd had medical training in the military and knew that alcohol can actually make an internal infection worse, so I took the second bottle of water, washed out the cut as best I could, and sprinkled it with sulfur powder.

Then because nothing else was available, I unlaced the shoestrings on my boots and tied them around my body and abdomen to stabilize the wound. I washed the blood off my head and treated that wound as well. It was important to get as much of the blood off as possible, to help keep insects away.

When I'd finished, I took a blanket from the overturned cot, wrapped up in it, and lay down on the floor.

What would Deborah do if I didn't make it? Deborah and I were divorced, but our son Terry needed my help. That's why I'd taken a job in Peru maintaining helicopters for the Bohling Brothers Oil Company—to take care of my son Terry's medical bills. He'd had a stroke and seizures not long after he'd had his appendix out, probably caused by a blood clot to the brain. They'd started him on an experimental drug that seemed to be working, but the hospital bills and ongoing medical treatment had decimated my savings account.

Besides, I'd promised my mother I'd take care of myself, that I'd come home. I was her only child, and there had been a special bond between us since my father's death.

I started to pray but stopped and thought that I should have been praying all my life instead of waiting until I was in trouble.

I'm either going to die or I'm going to live.

Chapter Two

WHEN I WOKE up the next morning, the sky that peeked through the open windows of the conex was changing its dark blue mantle to one of a paler hue, and the smell of smoke still hung in the air. The only sound I heard was the buzz of insects.

I needed to get out of there.

I had to move. I didn't have any idea how long it would be before the oil company realized something had happened and came to check it out, and I could be dead by then.

Another camp lay just 10 miles east of our camp.

I laughed. Just 10 miles?

The way I felt, it might as well be a hundred. But I had to try.

I scooted over to the first aid kit and searched through it again and found some vials of morphine, a big body bandage, and a suture kit. So I started untying the shoestrings I'd fastened around my body.

In my first aid training, I'd been told to stop the bleeding and prevent infection from getting inside. To wash the wound down, clean it up, put the sulfur powder on and shoot the patient with antibiotics if they were available. But my fingers felt big and clumsy as I untied the shoestrings and pulled my shirt away from the wound.

It was red and raw, still oozing blood. It looked really bad. For a moment my eyes welled up, and I was angry. Why had our camp been attacked? But I knew the answer to that. The terrorists wanted to ruin the country and didn't care who was hurt in the process.

Part of an intestine was exposed, but I didn't think it had been punctured. It didn't seem like I had any internal wounds. I didn't have the severe cramping or the severe thirst I'd always been told happens with internal wounds.

Then I took out the suture kit. Luckily the wound was down on my stomach, where I could get at it. I'd sewn up cuts before, in the military, so I scooted over where I could lean against the wall.

I thought about using one of the vials of morphine as a local anesthetic before starting but was afraid morphine might put me out and I'd never wake up.

So I just started sewing myself up. The first couple of stitches were a shock to my body, but then the brain's natural endorphins must have kicked in, because it wasn't so bad after that. I stitched a double layer—on the inside and on the outside—and sprinkled more sulfur power inside and applied iodine. When I finished, I was sweating and shaking.

The hardest part was bandaging myself up with the body bandage and tying the shoestrings around the bandage to help stabilize it. Then I just sat there for a while, catching my breath.

It would have been so easy to go back to sleep. My body was screaming at me to lie down and be still, but I had to get out of there. I had to get to the other camp. Of course, it might have been overrun as well, but it was a chance I had to take.

While I searched through the first aid kit for anything else that might be useful, Grandpa's voice kept echoing in my mind, almost like he was there.

"Never waste anything. Use what you have. Make due with what you've got."

I found some aspirin for pain. They'd taken my baseball cap, so I found a red bandana in the kit that was supposed to be used as a sling and tied it around my head to help protect it from insects. I found a scalpel that might come in handy, though my Swiss army knife was still in my pocket. And I found some safety pins and pinned my pants together where they'd been slashed.

Of course, to get to the next camp, I had to be able to walk. At least it would be easier to walk than to scoot through the mud.

The jungle of the Amazon Basin is a triple canopy jungle. Hardly anything can grow there because the sun doesn't reach the ground. It rains almost every day; but even when it isn't raining, water is dripping from the trees to the jungle floor, making it a muddy mess. So I had to be able to walk.

I'd pinned my pants together with safety pins, but I wasn't sure they would stay up, so I tied my shirt at the bottom and stashed the water bottles inside. The aspirin, the scalpel and the morphine vials I put in the pockets of my shirt and pants. Then dragging the blanket and the tarp, I scooted close to the cot that was still upright and leaned heavily against it while I got my feet under me and straightened my legs.

I was a little wobbly when I stood. A little dizzy. In fact, I thought I might fall, but I didn't. It didn't help that I could see myself in a mirror hanging by the door. A gaunt, thin-faced man with broad shoulders and intense blue eyes stared back at me, a man who looked decidedly older than my 48 years. Or maybe I just looked like a 48 year old man who'd been on a weekend bender. Blond hair stuck out from under my red bandana, and my glasses seemed to sit crooked across my nose. I grabbed hold of the blanket and the tarp and slowly, painfully, made my way to the door.

It might have been a normal day at camp. The conex sat at the east edge of the clearing, facing north, tucked back under the trees on that side. The sky revealed through the branches of those trees was bright now, and a quick glance at my watch told me it was almost 10:00 o'clock. Light was even seeping under the thickness of the jungle surrounding the camp. Except it was very quiet. I heard no voices, hardly any birds.

I stepped down out of the conex and looked around. The dead native still lay just beyond where I stood, his body bloated. I had a feeling there might be more bodies in the tall grass beyond him.

Grass grows very quickly in the Amazon Basin—almost immediately when the trees have been cleared away, as if leaping at the chance for life.

I could make out the charred remains of a few tents and could still smell smoke, though the putrid smell of rotting flesh was rapidly taking its place.

Some tree limbs lay beside the conex, so I decided to make a walking stick. Leaving the blanket and tarp at the door, I walked carefully to the limbs to check them out, carefully because my side protested every step.

One limb seemed about the right size. I trimmed it with my knife and used it as a crutch while looking around the camp, searching for anything that might be useful.

Almost everything had been blown up or burned. I was a pilot as well as a mechanic, but they'd shot up the control panel of the helicopter, including the radio. They'd even shot one of our dogs.

A couple of Americans were dead beside another conex, apparently trying to put up some kind of a fight.

When I'd finished my short trek around camp, I took stock of my resources. I had a pistol with 5 shots, my pocketknife, and the little scalpel I'd taken from the first aid kit.

I'd found some iodine tablets that I could use to purify water and had refilled the 2 water bottles. I'd also found part of a food kit, a hunter's food kit, with meals ready to eat.

Although I didn't have much of an appetite, I ate some of the malt balls and charms inside. There was also some aspirin. And there were the two morphine vials I could use if I had to, plus the tarpaulin and the blanket.

Our camp was just south of the Amazon River. The camp I wanted to reach was also close to the Amazon River. I didn't want to get too near the river because that's where the people and animals were. Possibly where the

Sendero were. My best bet was to keep the river far to my left and make my way through the jungle.

So looking at the sun (and keeping in mind that I was south of the equator and everything was reversed), I figured out which direction east was and started a slow walk toward the other camp.

Chapter Three

"Six . . . . Seven. . . . . Eight. . . . . Nine. . . . . . .Ten."
That made a hundred steps. I stopped, out of breath. When I'd first started walking, I had no way to judge how far I'd gone. So I started counting my steps, sticking out one finger at a time for every ten steps I took until I got to a hundred.

Then I would stop for a while, to catch my breath, to wipe the sweat out of my eyes and the flies and other insects out from behind my glasses before I started walking again.

The flies pestered, irritated me, but the small gnat-like insects were worse. Persistent little beasts, they swarmed every opening in my body—my ears—my nose—my mouth. I was constantly spitting them out.

I wanted to sit down. Oh, how I wanted to sit down. But I couldn't. I'd made that mistake once. It was too hard to get up again.

I thought I could hear the river. Although I didn't want to wander too far from it, I didn't want to get too close to it either. That's where the people were—along the river. But what kind of people would I run in to there—would they be friendly or unfriendly?

In my present condition, it would be foolish to take a chance.

I couldn't see the river from where I was. A wide, impenetrable wall of jungle growth ran along its edge, sealing me in and sealing the light out. Back inside the trees it was dark and hot, and the air was heavy with the smell of rotting compost. Water continually dripped from the trees above, making the ground wet and muddy.

There wasn't much undergrowth because the sun never touched the ground. I could walk with relative ease, as long as I avoided holes and rotting limbs and gnarled roots that stuck up out of the ground like knobby knees and elbows. I'd stumbled over one of those roots earlier and made the mistake of reaching out to a small tree nearby to break my fall and hundreds of stinging ants crawled up my arm.

Ants swarm the surfaces of small trees in the jungle because those trees secrete a sap that attracts them. They feed on the sap and in turn protect young trees from predators, but they sting like fire when they bite. When the trees are large enough, they no longer secrete sap and are safe to touch and get close to. I had learned all these things earlier, the first week after I'd arrived in camp, and learned them the hard way.

It was toss-up though. Was it better to fall to the ground and have to get to my feet or to break my fall by grabbing hold of a tree covered with those vicious little monsters? And I had done that a lot—fallen down—so many times that soon I'd be covered with mud and the insects would leave me alone.

I wiped the sweat off my face and put my glasses back on and felt something crawling down my back. I hoped it was just sweat. But I hastily raked insects out of the neck of my shirt and pulled my collar tighter before I started walking again, counting my steps again.

When I'd gone fifty, maybe sixty steps, I heard something--something other than the sounds of parrots, macaws, and other birds high up in the tops of the trees. A sound of someone or something moving through underbrush.

My first instinct was to hide. I felt exposed, standing as I was between tree trunks that suddenly seemed very far apart. A large tree grew some ten feet away, and I was tempted to move toward it. To put it between me and whatever was making the noise. But better judgment told me to freeze. To stay where I was and pray that the dim light under the triple canopy would hide me.

So slowly, carefully I took out the gun and stood very still, hardly breathing as the sound came closer; and I realized that what I was hearing was something crashing through the treetops. Then several monkeys peered down at me, little eyes, gleaming from little faces, studying me solemnly before scurrying off after their companions. Soon everything became quiet again, except for the buzzing of flies and cries of birds.

Sweat trickled down the sides of my face. I tucked the gun back under my shirt and wiped my face on my sleeve and wished for just a little wind to break the stillness of the heavy air.

A water rope hung from a nearby tree. Once I had seen a guy at camp taking a drink from one of those huge vines. He told me the vines could be used as a water source and showed me which ones to pick. The natives always used them for water when they went through the jungle, rather than carrying canteens.

A water rope looks kind of like a cane stalk because of the way it is sectioned. Each section holds a few tablespoons of a juice that tastes a little like grapefruit juice. So, before starting off again, I took out my Swiss Army

Knife, cut the vine open one section at a time, held the sections up to my mouth, and drank the tart liquid that trickled out.

One of my water bottles was empty. Though the other was almost full, I wanted to conserve that water as much as possible.

I had the iodine tablets and the river was nearby, but there was no way to make it through the growth at the river's edge without a machete. So I was dependent on the water I carried and the water I could find in the jungle. I made good use of the vine and decided to be on the lookout for more of the vines and use them as much as possible.

Then I started off over the muddy terrain again, counting again.

THE JUNGLE NEVER actually got light during the day; but at about 5:00 o'clock, it became noticeably darker. For some time I'd been looking for a place to stop when I saw a large tree that was forked at the bottom, where I could sit and be somewhat concealed. I hadn't seen any animals but the monkeys. I hadn't even seen any snakes. But predators do prowl the rain forest, even predators that aren't human.

After easing myself to the ground, I opened one of the hunter's food packs, and feasted on a dinner of peanut butter and crackers. Then I leaned back, so tired and hurting so much by then, that sleep came almost immediately.

Sometime in the middle of the night, I woke up to a blackness so complete that at first I thought I was blind—or in a cave with the lights out. Although the air was still heavy with moisture and the smell of compost, the temperature had decreased, at least a few degrees. The flies and gnats never took a nap though. They never slept.

I was thirsty but had to feel around to find the water bottle that lay beside me on the ground. Something, maybe a lizard, rustled the leaves and branches overhead.

I took a drink and closed my eyes again.

The next time I opened them, it was light. Birds chattered merrily in the treetops, and I thought I heard a motorboat passing by on the river. Was it the boat of a friend or a foe?

I drank some more water and ate a breakfast of malt balls then took out a package of pilot crackers—little round crackers that are very tasty. First I tried to open the package with my fingers, then my teeth. Finally I took out the Swiss Army Knife and stabbed though the foil wrapping. When I'd finished the meal, I got to my feet and started off again, counting by tens to a hundred.

I felt stronger that day and walking seemed easier, faster. About the middle of the second day, I came upon a path. I followed it and before long spotted red conexes and beyond them, a helicopter. I was pretty sure I'd made it to the other oil camp but still didn't know whether or not they'd been attacked. So I stopped back in the trees and watched while two men walked into view, their backs to me.

"—won't take that long once we get it started," one of them said before they walked away.

I was so relieved I almost cried. They were speaking English!

About fifteen feet inside the camp, a familiar figure came walking toward me, a big grin on his face. It was Hollywood Howard, an airplane and helicopter mechanic I'd worked with in Cambodia. He'd earned the name "Hollywood" not because he was from California but because of his habit of wearing sunglasses.

He looked me up and down. "Well, if it isn't Josh Phillips," he drawled. "We've got to quit meeting like this."

I'm surprised he recognized me—wearing a red bandana, face streaked with dirt. My clothes pinned together and hanging loosely on my lean 5'9" frame—bloody, muddy. Yes, I must have been a pretty sight by then.

"Okay by me." I laughed, even though it hurt.

Hollywood Howard took my arm to steady me and started walking me to one of the conexes.

"Looks like you mounted the wrong bull. What happened? Were you at that camp west of here, the one the *Sendero* hit?"

"Yeah."

"We thought everybody was dead. One of your engineers—a Limey, hid in the jungle during the attack. He came running in here two days ago, saying everyone else was dead or kidnapped."

"I was as good as dead."

"We flew over the camp and didn't see anyone. We were waiting on the army to arrive to go back in there for a closer look."

"Look who's here," he called to the guys I had seen earlier. They turned and looked at me in surprise. Hollywood Howard laughed. "It's Lazarus. Risen from the dead after three days."

I don't remember much of what happened next except that Hollywood Howard helped me into a conex and then to one of the cots. They gave me something for pain, cleaned me up a little, and checked my wounds; and everybody was calling me Lazarus because I had walked into camp three days after the attack.

They loaded me on a helicopter, and Hollywood Howard went with them when they transported me to a hospital in Peru. Then they flew me by plane to a hospital in Florida.

I HAD TWO visitors while I lay in that hospital bed, surrounded by clean, cold efficiency and the smell of disinfectant. The first was a minister who came to my room to talk with me because I'd put on the entrance form that I was a Protestant.

A small, nervous man, so small that he looked like he might have missed a promising career as a jockey, he seemed fascinated by my story, by the fact that everybody was calling me Lazarus.

He sat on the edge of his chair, like he wanted to be ready to jump up at a moment's notice and run out of the room. Not that he was unfriendly or anything, more like it was hard for him to sit still for long.

"Lazarus was given a second chance," he said, leaning forward. "Now you've been given a second chance. What are you going to do with it?"

I hadn't given the future much thought. I'd been having too much trouble with the present.

"What did Lazarus do with the rest of his life?"

That stumped him. He swallowed a couple of times and blinked his eyes. "The Bible doesn't say. Was he a mild man like the apostle John? Did he spend the rest of his life in contemplation?" He drummed his fingers against his knees. "We don't even know what his trade was. Was he a fisherman like Peter? A tax collector like Mathew? We don't know."

Then he had a thought that seemed to surprise him. "Of course, he could have been a soldier, like your name sake—like Joshua."

Maybe it was no coincidence that my second visitor was a representative of the State Department. When a citizen suffers, as I had suffered, at the hands of terrorists, the State Department sends someone to debrief that citizen. And maybe it was no coincidence that they sent Charles, a man I'd worked for briefly in Cambodia as a bean counter. Charles was a big man but every bit as edgy and intense as the minister had been. He didn't even attempt to sit down but stood during his entire dialogue with me and paced most of the time.

Finally, he stopped in the middle of the room and eyed me curiously.

"You got out of the military and became a policeman?"

"Yeah, for a while. While I was going to college."

"Then you were a school teacher. And became a mechanic?"

"Yes, aviation always—."

"How would you like to work for us again—in South America? How would you like to maintain helicopters and planes for the DEA?"

So that's how it happened. That's how my life changed overnight. That's how a simple schoolteacher, a simple airplane mechanic became involved in the war against drugs and communism in South America, involved in Operation Snowcap.

Part Two:
Dark World Revisited

Chapter Four

Somewhere over Nicaragua – Six Months Later

THE ONLY THING I could hear was the roar of the plane. The only thing I could feel was its vibration and the cold that always permeates planes and, if possible, all those who manage to get their feet very far off terra firma.

The pilot and co-pilot, vaguely illuminated by the lights on the control panel, hadn't said a word for over an hour and had hardly moved in all that time either. The flight engineer dozed in the chair beside me, his head leaning to one side at an odd angle. The other four members of the team sat at the front of the plane and appeared to be asleep too, though it was too dark to make them out clearly.

So there were seven team members in all, seasoned veterans in their 40's and 50's. The only one I'd met at the hotel in Mexico City was the pilot. And I'd only met him a couple of days before. I knew very little about the other men, except that a couple of them were guardians, former Navy Seals or Special Forces. Their job was to make sure the team got safely to wherever it was supposed to go. I also wondered if they were supposed to make sure nobody talked if they were captured.

We were riding in an old passenger plane, a four-engine Constellation much like a plane Howard Hughes had designed. It had been converted into a cargo plane, with a few seats left in the front and in the back. Talking was impossible, except over the headsets.

Just then Antonio, in the first passenger seat, opened his eyes and glanced over at me. A small, wiry man, originally from Spain, his black eyes flashed unbelievably bright in the dim interior of the plane and unbelievably penetrating. Antonio was one of the guardians. He was pleasant enough but never laughed when the others did. They all had nicknames, so Antonio was the one who suggested that they call me "Professor" because I'd taught school for a while.

Antonio's nickname was "Bond," as in James Bond. But I hadn't heard any of the men call him Bond, and he'd seemed embarrassed when I asked how he had acquired that moniker.

For the most part, despite the funny nicknames, they were a somber crew. That was the main difference I noticed right away between them and the men I'd served with years before in Cambodia. The men in Cambodia talked more, were more carefree. These men were all business; and I had the distinct impression, from the first time I'd met Antonio, just a few hours before, that the Spaniard had doubts about their new recruit.

I took a deep breath and released it slowly as Antonio turned away. Antonio wasn't the only one who had doubts.

Physically I was in good shape. I'd had plenty of time to recuperate from the wound in my side before going through rigorous training in Florida. I'd have to be in good shape, the pilot had told me the day I'd arrived. We would be making a two to three day hike through the country to some unspecified site.

Only a couple team members knew what the mission was. Perhaps they didn't want anyone who was captured to be able to give the enemy information. A comforting thought.

The pilot, Randy Tanner, was a slender man who looked like he'd stepped out of an African safari movie. He wore a leather fedora hat and a black leather jacket and had a mustache that wiggled up and down at the sides when he talked.

He'd made a production of the secrecy of the mission. We'd met in the bar the day I'd arrived in Mexico City then had gone to his room to talk.

As soon as we entered, Randy gestured for me to remain still and be quiet. Puzzled, I stood in the center of the room, while he took out a little device and made a show of slipping around checking for bugs. Then he moved the table away from the window and turned the radio on to Mexican music. He set the volume up so loud that it made talking difficult but added a definite Latino flavor to the meeting.

He told me we were flying to a site where we'd make an off-airport landing. Then we'd walk for 3 to 4 days to another site. I was told to cut the labels out of all my clothes and to eat only local food, so I wouldn't smell like an American.

"Don't use toothpaste or American after-shave or deodorant—only use local products. And no girlfriends, Josh," Randy said sternly, as if that might be a problem for me.

"Don't make any friends period. The only people you need to talk to are the clerks. Don't get drunk or make a spectacle of yourself in any way. Blend in. And get plenty of rest. You'll need it."

22

I nodded. That certainly didn't sound too hard.

"Do you have any questions?"

I had a million questions, but Randy had already made it clear that he couldn't really give me the answers I wanted.

"I know you can't tell me anything about the mission itself, but can you tell me anything else about my role? About what I will be expected to do?"

"You're a mechanic, but, I understand, you're also a pilot. We like your skills. You'll be on the flight crew. You can help take care of the plane." Then Randy leaned forward across the table and lowered his voice. "But the main reason you were chosen," he said, with a Mexican band playing cheerfully in the background, "is because you scored very high on the rifle range."

My stomach tightened. That's what I was afraid of. Grandpa had been right. Aiming at sticks paid off. But now I was wishing I'd aimed at bottles or cans. What kinds of jobs did the State Department ask people to do? Did they want me to shoot someone? Assassinate someone? I wasn't sure I could do that.

The next day I went with Randy to the airport. Oddly enough, the plane we were taking wasn't sitting in a hanger. It was outside—exposed to the elements and anyone who might wander by.

It was an old Constellation that had been modified, with beta control props, which are reversing propellers to help the plane stop in a short time. We did an ordinary mechanical inspection. But the Constellation is not an ordinary plane. It has four engines, with 36 spark plugs to clean and check for each engine. That made 144 spark plugs in all.

We also checked the fuel and the oil and turned on various power systems. Then we searched the plane for anything that would give away its identification, such as US registration marks, and removed them. The engine number and date sticker had already been removed.

"Big Bird, Ground Team," a Donald Duck voice came over his headset, bringing me back to the present. The message came over a single side band radio. You can communicate all over the world with them, but they distort the voice. Everyone sounds like Donald Duck.

"Big Bird," Randy answered.

"Divert. Divert. We have unfriendlies near the landing strip."

"I understand. Divert. Divert."

The pilot turned in his seat to look back at me and the flight engineer, who had opened his eyes and was rubbing his neck like it hurt. "You hear that?"

"Yeah," I said, "what does it mean?"

"Somebody must have alerted them. They've probably got troops waiting for us at our first landing site. So we're going to another landing site."

Randy took out a map, and he and the co-pilot bent over it, plotting a new course. The flight engineer, everybody called him Flash Gordon, gave me a grim grin and scooted down in his seat and closed his eyes again. Flash was a big man with a round boyish-type face that made him look much younger than his thinning hair and the skin on the backs of his hands revealed him to be.

After a while Randy said they were going to a landing site located several miles from the first landing site.

Unfriendlies. For the first time the danger that lay ahead was all too real. There were men on the ground waiting to kill me.

And all too soon the plane began to loose altitude. I followed Randy's instructions to lower the flaps 10 degrees to slow the plane, and the word came to get ready for the landing.

As I prepared for a crash landing, I asked myself what I was doing there, going into the unknown again. Into that dark world again, a world I thought I'd left behind forever when I left Cambodia and Viet Nam.

Chapter Five

I BRACED MYSELF as the plane bounced and rolled, small trees thumping against its belly. Finally, the tail slid to the right; and the plane shuddered and stopped. All things considered it was a very good landing.

Randy stood. "Okay, gather up your civilian clothes and your equipment and get out."

I grabbed up my things and followed a couple of other guys off the plane. I was wearing the army fatigues of another country, made of light, tiger-stripped cloth that looked vaguely like the uniforms of Nicaragua. But I wasn't sure. We had all changed into fatigues shortly after we'd boarded the plane.

I was carrying a rifle, but it had a laser on it. So I probably wouldn't be expected to assassinate anyone. A couple of the other guys had laser guns too. The rebels were probably planning a bombing raid, and the laser guns would direct the bombs to their targets.

When I exited, I found myself in a big, open field, the air warm and humid, the sky just beginning to get light. It was a rough area, rough and hilly. A few small trees were scattered across the field with more trees around edges. Beyond the field lay the dark shape of a single canopy jungle.

We'd damaged the plane. Randy had put the wheels down to cut the risk of fires and explosions. Though the wheels were intact, one tire was flat, and we'd torn up one wing tip and nicked the flaps and the propellers. We wouldn't be flying out right away, not on that plane.

"We've got to wait for the other guardians," Randy told us. "So if you want to smoke or chew, do it now. It will be the last time you'll be able to for a few days."

A couple of the guys lit up cigarettes.

But they didn't have long to smoke before the dark shadows of four men emerged from the trees at the edge of the field and came up at a run.

"You're going to have to hurry," the first one said. "They're coming."

"Okay, bring your civilian clothes over here," Randy gestured at us to take our clothes to the plane's fuel drains.

The co-pilot pulled the drains, and we soaked our clothes with gasoline then carried them to the door of the plane and one of the guardians placed them inside.

Four men in all had joined the team. Two of those men were guardians and two were natives. The natives strapped on packs so they could help carry the equipment, and they and Randy led off across the field. The rest of us had put on our packs and were already following close behind when the guardians tossed grenades in the plane, cutting the silence and darkness with explosions and orange flares of heat and light.

We walked at a fairly quick pace through grass that was up to our knees, leaving a trail a schoolgirl could follow.

Soon the sun came out, and it got hot.

After blowing up the plane, the guardians had disappeared into the jungle. The rest of us walked at a normal pace for the first few hours. But soon Antonio came up at a fast trot, his face streaked with sweat.

"You're going to have to go faster," he said. "They're getting close."

"Okay, this is what we're going to do," Randy said, as we all gathered around him. "We'll jog fifty paces, then walk fifty paces. Let's go!"

We took off jogging. Sometimes I got winded. But I knew that if I kept moving, soon I'd get enough oxygen back into my system to breathe normally again. If I stopped to sit down and gasp for breath, I'd be lost. After a while, my legs started to cramp; and I got a stitch in the side that had been wounded. But I kept walking or jogging, and soon the pain went away.

The sun rose higher and became s furnace against my head, and the straps of the pack began to cut into my shoulders. Sweat ran down my face and neck and stung my eyes, and the insects came at me in droves. Always the insects.

We kept up the quick pace—jogging fifty paces and walking fifty paces—for two hours straight. At first everybody was keeping up, but toward the end of that two hours we began to wear out—and string out. It wasn't easy at times, but I managed to stay in the middle of the pack.

Finally, we got to a little river, and Antonio joined us again and told us we'd be walking in the river, going downstream for a while. I eagerly followed the others in. It was only about knee deep. But now we'd be able to travel without leaving such an obvious trail. And now we'd get a little relief from the heat.

First we walked downstream for about 100 yards; then we turned around and walked back up the stream in the opposite direction—back toward the people who were coming. We passed our entry point and walked farther upstream, until we came to a place with a lot of brush on both sides of the river, brush that actually extended into the water at the edge.

Antonio gave the signal to stop and circle the area. The men ahead of me fanned out at either side of the river. Randy took up a position about 10 yards upstream in rocks and brush close to the bank to my right, and one of the native men walked farther upstream and headed to a position across from Randy.

I went back downstream to a log that poked up out of the river in some brush on the left, then gratefully pulled off my pack and laid it on top the log and put my rifle on top. As I took out some food, I watched a dark-skinned man, introduced earlier as Underdog, one of the guardians, slipping through the brush on the opposite shore.

Underdog looked part Indian, with sleek, black hair that was long and straight and secured at the back of his head with a rubber band. He smiled at me, revealing white, even teeth before disappearing between the bushes that grew out into the river.

Upstream Randy was still standing and drinking from his canteen, but the other men were out of sight.

I got my own canteen, faced away from the river, watching the shore, and took a few sips of water, careful not to drink too much too quickly because that might cause stomach cramps.

Then I gratefully sank into a couple a feet of cool water to sit on the river's rocky bottom behind the log, with the water coming halfway up my chest. A thick stand of trees and brush edged the shore, blocking my view. But they blocked the view of anyone approaching from that direction too.

I took a white stimulant pill so I wouldn't fall asleep and chewed a few squares of dried beef jerky and ate a few malt balls and squinted my eyes against the attacks of the insects that swarmed me.

At first the water in the river was cool against my skin, but after I'd sat in it for a while, it felt tepid, almost warm. During rainy season it would be cold, and the river would have been too deep to navigate easily. It was about 75 to 100 feet wide at that particular point, with a rocky bottom that was clearly visible. The people tracking us would be studying the bottom of the river, looking for scuffmarks, places where boots had disturbed the moss and silt on those rocks.

Occasionally a minnow approached me and nibbled at my clothes, then moved on. And once a small bird with brilliant green plumage landed on the far end of the log and cocked its head at me before flying off to the opposite shore.

For the most part I played the part of a statue, but I had to get to my feet a couple of times to keep my legs from getting stiff. Once when I stood,

Flash Gordon slid out from his hiding place, only his head and shoulders visible above the water, and gestured for me to get down. Then he pointed downstream at the shore on his own side of the river.

I slipped noiselessly back into the water and watched the opposite shore. I couldn't see anything but soon smelled cigarette smoke. You can smell it half a mile away. That's why we weren't allowed to smoke. Then I heard the sound of people passing, talking quietly in Spanish among themselves.

Although I only knew a little Spanish, I tensed, listening for words, and turned every so slightly toward the sound. But thankfully the brush was too thick to make out where these people were or what they were doing. I assumed the men pursuing us had crossed the river and were searching for sign on the opposite shore, searching for me.

Soldiers are, by and large, lousy trackers. But sometimes they have trackers with them, men like the guardians on our own team, who can read tracks like they are reading a book and who themselves leave almost no tracks at all.

I remained rigid, hardly daring to move long after the sounds had faded away.

Then I just sat there, how many hours, I didn't know. I ate a few malt balls, and when it got dark, put on my night goggles. I started getting sleepy again, so I took another stimulant pill. The stimulant pills not only keep you awake, they decrease your appetite. So I didn't fell much like eating.

Finally, when it was very dark, the guardians came walking up the river. One of them, whom I later learned was Willie, a Seminole Indian from Florida, moved close to me. "It's safe to go downstream again. We're heading out."

I stood and put my pack on, grateful to be able to stand up again, to walk again. I almost caught up with Flash Gordon, and could see a couple of other men not too far ahead of us, who had started walking downstream. We all moved quietly, keeping to the center of the stream and being careful not to splash water, only lifting our feet a few inches off the bottom of the river.

After we'd walked for about two or two and a half hours, Willie appeared beside me like a phantom and leaned in close. "You're going to have to be extremely quiet for a while," he said softly. "Stay together. Move very slowly and carefully. Don't talk"

Then he slipped back into the shadows.

Before long, I could smell smoke, and though I couldn't see anything because of the darkness and the bushes along the shore and though I didn't hear anything, I assumed we were passing by the enemy camp.

After creeping along at a snail's pace for thirty minutes, Antonio told us to move forward more quickly.

We continued to walk in the river until about an hour before sunrise, when we stopped on gravel shoals. We piled some brush up—to give ourselves a little cover—then sat down or lay down.

My body was numb with fatigue. I had no trouble dozing off.

"Time to wake up, professor."

I felt a hand on my shoulder and opened my eyes to find Flash Gordon sitting beside me grinning.

"You got a class in about ten minutes. So you better eat something while you can." Flash took a sip from his coffee cup.

"Have you got coffee there?"

"Yeah, cold coffee. We can't have any fires here, so I just mixed some coffee with water. It's better than nothing."

"By the way," I said, as I took out my own cup, "where are we?"

Flash looked surprised that I didn't know, but we hadn't exactly had much chance to talk.

"We're in Nicaragua," the tall, dark-skinned man sitting beside Flash spoke up.

"Have you met Pretty Boy?" Flash asked, and the man grinned at the name.

"Heraldo Cervantes," he said, extending his hand.

"Josh Phillips."

Heraldo or Pretty Boy had steel gray hair and was a handsome man in spite of a scar that ran along his right cheekbone.

"Pretty Boy knew where we were the minute we landed. This is his territory."

"Not any more," the dark man said bitterly. "Ortega stole my family's land and everything else we had."

Nobody said anything for a while. The crimes the communists committed against the citizens of the country were well known. I couldn't imagine how it would be to have everything you'd worked for stolen by the government.

"Do you still have family here?"

Pretty Boy shook his head. "Maybe a cousin or two. If they're still alive. The communists killed my parents and two of my brothers."

The Nicaraguan government was under Ortega's control. His government, the Sandinista government, was a ruthless, communist dictatorship, where the "welfare of the people" was an excuse for those in charge to rob and destroy.

"I guess the Sandinistas have killed a lot of people in Nicaragua."

Pretty Boy nodded. "They executed 8,000 people in the first three years they were in power, and that's not counting the 15,000 Miskito Indians they captured and tortured.

"My parents and some of the workers on our ranch were lined up in the street and shot. They told everybody they were shot trying to escape, but a friend of mine saw what happened. One of my brothers just disappeared like thousands of other people. But my youngest brother ended up in prison." Pretty Boy's jaw tightened, and he turned away. "He's dead now though."

I'd heard stories about what happened to the people the Sandinistas imprisoned. They were beaten and tortured with electric shocks and kept in cells too small to even sit down in. The cells had no sanitation, and prisoners were often deprived of food and water.

"Aren't the Nicaraguans having another election soon?" Flash asked.

"Yes, and this time it's going to be different." Pretty Boy smiled, his eyes hard, like he knew more than he was saying. "Last time Ortega rigged the elections and used brute force and fear to make everybody vote for him. He's been doing that again. But this time it's going to be different."

Nobody talked for a while.

The sky was clear, softening to a pale blue, the air fresh and clean. Insects and birds sang, and the river moved lazily past. Looked like a good morning to be out fishing—except for the mosquitoes.

I ate some more beef jerky cubes and a little candy and drank coffee and thought about what might lie ahead.

The soldiers who committed the atrocities Pretty Boy described were the same soldiers that were following us now. Torture and imprisonment was the fate that awaited us if we were caught—only it would be worse for us, because the United States government wouldn't acknowledge our presence in the country. We were ex-patriots or ex-pats, with no apparent ties to the United States. Our families would have no idea where we were. We would just disappear, and the Sandinistas could do whatever they wanted with us.

Soon we received the order to move out again. I felt surprisingly refreshed after only about an hour of rest. We started back down the river, moving at a steady pace, but still being careful not to splash or make any unnecessary noise.

I wondered about the mission as we moved through the water and wondered if the United States had sent covert teams to Nicaragua to help the people before. I knew my government couldn't police the whole world, but sometimes it seemed like they were awfully slow to help people who were being abused by their own governments.

We'd walked for about 30 maybe 40 minutes when we heard several shots, coming from behind, maybe a mile or two away. We quickened our pace, without being told; and soon Antonio entered the river and was talking to the men downstream, and I could tell, from the way their demeanor changed that something had happened, something bad.

Pretty Boy waited for Flash and me to catch up to him.

"They shot Willie," he said.

Chapter Six

"They killed Willie?" Flash stared at him in disbelief. "How did they do that? He moves like a ghost."

"He ran right into a couple of them and stepped in a hole as he was trying to get away." The man's blue eyes flashed anger, or hatred. "They shot him about twenty times. But he took a couple of them with him. Antonio says move faster. They're getting close."

Then as most of us hurried on downstream as fast as we could in water that was up to our waists now, Antonio and Underdog put anti-personnel bombs behind us on the bed of the river. These bombs are about the size of golf balls. When you step on them, they can do some damage, plus they make quite a pop.

After about 45 minutes the first of those bombs went off, followed by two more pops. It sounded like our pursuers were within a mile or a mile and a half of us.

For about half an hour we made pretty good time because the water was only up to our knees. Then it deepened again. Still we pushed forward, going as quickly as we could until we came to an area where the terrain along the river was made up of hard clay, covered in fairly short grass.

The guardians motioned us to the shore and told us to take a short break and change our shoes and socks because we were leaving the river.

I just sat down on the ground for a minute or two and watched the others taking their extra pairs of shoes from their packs, taking out a little food, or just staring into space as I was. We were a ragged looking crew.

The mood of the group had changed since Willie's death. Nobody was even smiling.

I unlaced my boots and peeled off my soggy socks then dried my feet and powdered them before putting on a clean, dry pair. I had no appetite, but didn't know how long it would be before we would take another break, so I forced myself to drink some water and eat some candy and a couple of squares of dried beef.

A few minutes later Antonio told us to move out, down a path beside the river. We moved at a fast clip again—running fifty paces then walking fifty paces—just as we had before. The path was well traveled, covered with tracks, and we were wearing the boots of the country, but a good tracker could tell the difference.

Toward evening, Antonio and one of the other guardians came in and motioned us into the jungle along the right side of the trail. Then they led us way back in the trees until we came to a little clearing that had been picked out as a campsite. Antonio said the soldiers were no longer following us, so we could finally get some rest and have fires.

We set up gun positions. Then I helped Flash Gordon and a couple of the other guys camouflage the area by filling in openings in the ceiling with leafy tree limbs. Finally, I sat down with my back against a tree and had rice cakes and hot chocolate for dinner.

None of us were particularly hungry, but everyone ate something. There was very little talking. We had hammocks we could string between trees, but nobody bothered to put one up. We just wrapped up in our ponchos and lay on the ground, using our packs as pillows.

The next morning, after a brief breakfast, some of us had to put on makeup—that is, we had to darken our faces, so they'd blend in better. I had blond hair sticking out from under my hat, but blond hair was not all that unusual in South America. My skin, on the other hand, was far too pasty. I had to cover it with something anyway, because I burned so easily.

We were on the outskirts of Managua, Nicaragua's capital city. Randy quickly outlined where each of us was to go in the city and where we were to meet when everything was over. Then we got back on the trail, running again, not because the enemy was behind us but because we needed to hurry to get to the target area.

Before long we came to a road, and one of the guardians motioned us to exit the road on the left.

Then Randy took over. He and one of the other men brushed out the tracks where we'd left the tail and walked into the trees, but they didn't dust the area or cover it with leaves or anything. Any good tracker would recognize the brush marks for what they were.

"That should be a dead giveaway," I said, under my breath, and Underdog, a guardian who was directly in front of me, turned and grinned.

But what came next was a little bizarre. We were getting close to Managua; so it was time for us to split up and go to our specific positions. I would be going into the city with Underdog.

"Walk in single file," Randy said. "And I want each man to step in the footprints of the man in front of him."

We lined up and went forward about 100 yards.

"Okay, now stop and go backwards, and step in the same footprints."

A couple of people muttered, but we all did what he asked—to the best of our ability. Then when we'd gone about 20 yards Randy stopped us and started us in another direction, and a couple of people split off from the rest of the group and headed for town.

We walked forward about 100 yards again, then back-tracked a short way again, lost two members of our party, and started off in still another direction. We must have spent four or five hours going through this strange exercise.

For the most part we were in slash and burn farmland, farmland abandoned after all the nutrients had been sucked from the soil. Trees edged fields and grew thick along the rivers and streams.

So there we were, mostly keeping to the tree line and walking like mechanical ducks in a row. If I hadn't been so tense by then, in anticipation of what lay ahead, I might have died laughing at how comical we probably looked.

But in fact, it made me angry at first. I knew Randy was trying to make it look to anyone following like there were single trails that led to various points in a field or in the trees then and just disappeared. But this particular maneuver was too time consuming. I couldn't see why we didn't just dawn moccasins to travel across country and/or follow a path that paralleled the roads.

Flash was directly behind me and snickered once when we started our backward maneuver. When I glanced back at him, he leaned forward. "He's a Company Man," he said quietly.

"Randy?"

He nodded, and Underdog turned, grinning from ear to ear.

That seemed to explain it, as far as they were concerned. Randy worked for the CIA, and everybody knew they used strange methods.

Underdog and I were one of the last to split from the group. We made our way to a fairly busy road and just walked beside it, because it was not at all unusual for a couple of soldiers to be walking down the road. But we were running late because of the dance we'd done in the woods.

Underdog kept looking at his watch.

"Are we going to make it to our target area?"

He shook his head. "Not at this rate."

"Maybe we should hitch-hike."

"I got a better idea."

Pretty soon we spotted a taxicab coming up behind us, and Underdog waved his arms at it.

When it pulled to the side of the road, Underdog approached the driver's window and began to talk to him about the fare. Underdog was a Navaho Indian, but he spoke perfect Spanish.

He must have spent five or ten minutes arguing with the driver. The driver would name a price, and Underdog would protest. He used the word "bandito" several times.

So they kept up the argument for a while, hands flailing the air before they finally agreed. Then Underdog and I got in the taxicab and rode into the city. I kept my mouth shut and let my partner do all the talking. Soon traffic filled the streets as in any major city, but we made it to within a short distance of our assigned points in good time and paid the driver maybe 50 cents in his currency.

As the taxi drove off, I turned to Underdog and shook my head. "Is this what the big argument was about?" We had each been given a packet containing the currency of several different countries, as well as four gold coins that were Canadian and South African and four silver coins that were Mexican, the coins packed in bubble packs so they wouldn't rattle. Thus, we weren't exactly hurting for money.

Underdog grinned. "He would have been suspicious if I hadn't bartered with him."

Then Underdog walked off, blending into the crowd. He also had a rifle, but he didn't have a laser on his rifle. I figured that my partner's job was to watch and protect, but whatever he did, he did from a distance.

I went to my assigned spot—across from a government building that was one of the targets of the attack and sat down by the corner on some steps that led down to a basement. I was carrying my laser gun, which looks like a little rifle, but soldiers carrying rifles weren't all that uncommon in Managua. Nobody paid any attention to me.

Before long I heard the drone of several small aircraft approaching the area.

My stomach tightened as I stood and pointed the laser beam at the building, at the spot I'd been told to aim at. One of the aircraft dropped a bomb. I saw the bomb fall and watched it track in on the laser beam directly to the target.

It hit with a concussion blast. Dirt and dust blew out, followed by a swooshing sound as the air rushed in and the fire rushed back out. Other bombs were hitting the area as well, and the building cracked and started to crumble.

Of course, there was chaos on the street now. People running out of the buildings. The sound of gunfire and people yelling. Some of those around me were trying to see what was going on while others took cover.

I walked through the crowds to my next position—about two blocks away. A police car and a fire truck screamed down the street and a soldier stood on the sidewalk shooting at planes that were out of range.

Then I rounded a corner and almost ran into an army officer coming from the other direction.

I started to brush past him, but he grabbed my arm. The laser gun fell to the sidewalk, and my heart missed a beat.

Chapter Seven

THE OFFICER GRIPPED my arm and yelled something in Spanish. So I just froze, and he looked past me to the soldier in the street who was still firing and released me and started yelling at the soldier. I grabbed up the laser gun and lost myself in the crowd.

I arrived at my second position just in time to hear the planes approaching again then took aim and held the gun as steady as possible while, once again, a bomb tracked its beam to the target. The explosions that followed created complete chaos on the street.

People ran for cover, yelling, cursing. People shot at airplanes—or shot just to be shooting. More police cars, fire trucks, and ambulances arrived. I tossed the laser gun in a trashcan and walked away from the area. At one point an officer in a passing car saw me and gave me an order. But I didn't know what the order meant. But, then, nobody else was following orders either. I just took off in the opposite direction—heading away from the scene.

An hour or so after the battle I was walking along a road on the outskirts of town when I someone behind me called my name.

"Hey, Joshua, hold up."

It was Flash and Underdog.

We met Randy and a couple of other guys at the pick up point, and soon all the others came in too. We hadn't lost one person.

We waited in some trees and brush at the edge of a clearing while the guardians called to have the team picked up. It was the first time we'd used the radio. Within 20 minutes Russian helicopters landed.

The Russians only had two things to export—oil and weapons, so the State Department had bought some Russian helicopters and sent them to pick us up, because it was much less suspicious that way.

The helicopters took us to a little hotel where we took showers, changed clothes, and picked up our ID's. Then we flew back to Mexico City on a passenger plane.

On the plane I sat next to a tall, beefy man in his late 50's or early 60's, probably the oldest member of the team. His nickname was "the Reverend." I figured maybe he'd been a preacher in his early life. Still I was a surprised when he took a small New Testament out of his shirt pocket and started reading it.

Something had been nagging at me since the attack.

"Does it bother you," I asked him, "that we probably hurt innocent people today?"

He put his head back against his seat and looked out the window of the plane for a moment.

"Okay," he finally said, "this is the way I see it. What the government is doing is wrong. They have hurt and will hurt a lot more innocent people than we hurt today. And they do it intentionally."

He turned back to his Bible. "Besides, God has His own ways of protecting the ones that need protecting."

When we got to Mexico City, we all met at the hotel bar to drink a special toast to Willie. The service we had that night was likely the only service he would get. Willie's name would be added to a plaque in Panama, a plaque that listed all the names of those killed in our special line of work.

Antonio, because he knew Willie the best, did most of the talking. He said Willie was a high-school dropout who had been raised by his grandmother.

"He was a Navy Seal in Vietnam. He joined up because he said his grandmother was a mean, old woman. She's dead now, so he doesn't have any family to grieve over him, except for a couple of aunts and some cousins; and they probably don't care. They never wrote him or anything."

"What about his parents?" Pretty Boy asked.

"His mother died when he was young. I don't know about his father. He never mentioned him, and I never asked."

Underdog frowned. "I thought he was married."

"Yeah, he was for a while, when he was in the Navy. Maybe about fifteen years."

"Didn't he have some children?"

Antonio shrugged. "Yeah, he had two. But then his wife remarried. It was a nasty divorce, and his wife even claimed at one point that they weren't really his kids."

I had a couple of drinks and just sat there for a while, talking some, but mainly listening to the others and wondering about them. From what they were saying, most ex-pats were loners—unmarried, at present. Most of them had gone to college and trained as pilots, mechanics and technicians. They all seemed to have military backgrounds, and most of them had served in Vietnam twenty years before as civilian contractors or with the military.

So we had something else in common too—the gray in our hair.

Later, Flash went to the bar and was trying to make friends with one of the barmaids. He wasn't having any luck though, so I joined him.

Antonio wouldn't tell me how he'd earned the name "Bond," so I asked Flash.

"Because he's the nearest to being James Bond of any guy in the outfit. I guess you know he was originally from Spain. Well, his sister and his aunt and uncle made the mistake of going to Cuba when Antonio came to the U.S. His sister got married there and had a couple of boys, and, of course, those boys eventually got old enough to be drafted." He paused and glanced over at me.

I knew what was coming. "Old enough to serve in Castro's mercenary army?" Castro sent his soldiers all over the world as mercenaries. Then he collected the pay for their services.

"Antonio didn't want his nephews to die in Africa fighting somebody else's war, so he went to Cuba alone. He gained entry to the country and got his whole family out within a week. That's how he earned the name 'Bond.'"

"Wow." I thought about what an extraordinary feat that was. I wondered about the other men. "You know, I've been puzzled. These men seem to be non-conformists, but I don't think I've met anyone from California or New York. That's where I'd expect non-conformists to be from."

"Nah, we rarely have ex-pats from California. They're crazy people. And New Yorkers?" He laughed. "They argue too much. We get rid of people right away who like to argue. We can't afford to fight with each other. We'd end up killing each other. Most of our people are from Oklahoma, Texas, Missouri, and Alaska. Once in a while from Georgia or another southern area."

I glanced around the room and wondered how many other James Bond stories they could tell. They were a tough group, but I could hardly recall hearing a profane word the whole time I'd been with them.

But then they didn't have anything to prove. That was another difference between the young guns I'd served with in Vietnam 20 years before and these men—the seasoned professionals.

How would I measure up? I'd had no real problems on this assignment, but what about the next assignment? What would the next assignment be?

It came almost immediately after arriving back at the base in Florida—the news that I was to go back to Peru, not as an employee of an oil company, but as part of a crew that would replace some men whose plane had been blown out of the air by drug traffickers.

The drug traffickers needed some new targets to shoot at.

Part Three:
Welcome to Lima

Chapter Eight

Lima, Peru – One Month Later

THE AIRPORT IN Lima was deceptively modern and attractive. I made the trip with Scott, one of the people I'd trained with in Florida. Scott, a tall, lanky guy with a sun-darkened complexion and light brown hair, was from Montana. He had grown up on a ranch where his nearest neighbor was miles away. An easy-going guy, nothing much seemed to faze him. We exchanged cowboy stories.

The plane landed at the Lima airport at about 11:00 at night. The site manager was supposed to meet us but hadn't arrived. So we went on over to the baggage area to collect our luggage. When it finally appeared on the conveyor belt, I pulled out one-dollar bills to pay some of the locals to help tote them. Usually, a dollar a bag is a fair price for such assistance, but not this time. Pandemonium broke out.

Immediately a couple of kids about fourteen or fifteen started fighting over one of my bags—grabbing, pushing each other, finally hitting each other. Meanwhile two other kids attacked a guy who had picked up one of Scott's bags.

"Now, hold on!" Scott tried to protect the first guy and almost got hit himself.

"Hey!" I yelled and threw the dollar bills into the air.

As they were scrambling for the money, we took the luggage and set it against the wall.

Scott chuckled. "What were you trying to do, partner, get us killed?"

I held up my hand as a couple of guys started toward the bags again. "Now, leave them alone! Don't touch them!"

I'm not sure how long we waited before we decided to do something about getting a ride to the hotel. We didn't see any taxis out front and knew only a few words in Spanish between us. Finally, I left Scott to guard the luggage and went to find someone who could tell us how to get a taxi.

The airport was pretty much closed up, but I found a man behind one of the counters with a broom in his hands. He knew a little English, and he finally seemed to understand what I wanted.

"No, no," he said. "Very dangerous. Much trouble here. Taxis don't like go airport. Very dangerous."

"Then how do visitors get out of the airport?"

He shook his head and turned away, as if that answered the question.

What had we gotten ourselves into?

Fortunately, the site manager arrived just as I made it back to Scott. A fleshy man, who perspired a lot, he introduced himself as Carson but didn't apologize for being late and certainly didn't seem happy to see his two new employees.

"Now, come on," he said impatiently. "We can't stand around in here. My pickup is outside the doors in the street. Got to get back to it."

He didn't offer to help us with our bags, so we loaded up and went after him as quickly as we could.

"What's going on here?" I asked. "Why don't taxis come to the airport?"

"Yeah, taxis can't come out here, but they expect me to come out here just about every night." Carson took my bag and put it in the back of his truck. "They've hired a bunch of extra men, and I've had to make this trip almost every night because none of you jokers can come in on the same flight."

I glanced around. The area around the airport didn't look that bad. "Is this a bad part of town?"

He laughed dryly and threw one of Scott's suitcases on top of mine. "This is Kail, only the worst section of Lima."

He tried to take another of Scott's bags, and Scott stopped him. "Hold it, partner, I can do that."

Carson glared at him. "Well, hurry up."

We got in the pickup. He locked his door and told us to do the same. Then he started putting on a pair of leather gloves.

"This part of Lima is Sin City—prostitution, drugs, smuggling, murders every night. It's the poorest part of the city except for the people in grass huts. You have to leave here by limousine or armored car."

"This doesn't look like an armored car," Scott said.

"No." Carson cast a fearful look at the road behind and then peeled out of his parking place. "I drive fast," he yelled. "If I drive fast enough, the Drones won't shoot at me and hit me."

"That's reassuring," Scott muttered.

"Who are the—?" I was going to ask him who the drones were, but we went flying down the street. He was occupied with his driving, and I was busy watching houses and parked cars and buildings and intersections pass by at the speed of light.

Finally, we made it to a more affluent part of the city, Miraflores; and our driver seemed to relax a little, though he was still going too fast.

"Peru is in a Civil War," he said. "The *Sendero Luminoso* is fighting the government and the Le Drones are fighting everybody."

"Who are the Le Drones?"

"Thieves and murderers, and they roam the streets, killing and robbing." He glanced over at me. "I thought you'd been in Peru before. Thought you knew what you were getting into."

"I was working for an oil company. We were treated like VIP's. We landed at another part of the airport and were transported immediately to the Sheridan and then to the site. I didn't have much contact with the local people. Besides I was only in Peru for a couple of months."

He stopped the car at an intersection and sighed. "Well, you're not a VIP any more."

After wiping perspiration from his brow, he glanced furtively up and down the street before making a left turn and gunning the truck back up to speed.

"We pay the police to protect us in this part of the city," he continued, "but still you can't be too careful. The Le Drones are organized to steal. One of their favorite methods is to catch somebody by himself and surround him and try to rip his pockets off to get whatever falls down on the ground. Then you'll be lucky if they don't knock you down and knife you or kick you to death."

Lima is an ancient city—founded by the conquistadors, but Miraflores looked very modern. We passed movie theatres, cafes, and businesses.

He screeched to a halt at a hotel, where he said we were expected; and we jumped out of the truck and snatched our luggage out of the back before he could throw it out into the street.

"Don't leave the hotel. We're having a meeting at the embassy in a couple of days. We'll send an armored car for you."

"Are we safe here?" I asked.

"Sure, nobody knows we're using this hotel. Keep a low profile." He got in his pickup and left before Scott and I even got through the doors.

The hotel we entered was fairly new, a Spanish style hotel, about 10 stories high. All the rooms contained balconies that faced a center atrium, and the exterior windows of my room gave me a board view of the ocean.

But the appearance of the hotel was also deceptive. Though it looked modern, there was no heat or air conditioning. The nights were cold, but the hotel only provided one thin blanket. We were on water rationing too.

I could only use water (multi-colored water) for a short time each day and could only use it to shower.

At the hotel Scott and I met up with some other guys who had just arrived. I'd known a few of these guys when I'd worked for the Department of State in Southeast Asia. It was like old-home week, because we hadn't seen each other in such a long time—about 20 people in all. A fairly big group. I wondered just how many men had been killed in the plane that had been shot down.

The next day Flash, Scott, and I went up on the roof to have something to eat and lounge around by the swimming pool. A nice restaurant and bar stood at one end of the pool, with cooked steak and bananas on the menu. We found a table under the covered patio area and ordered dinner. In our rooms we'd each found a card for a free pisco sour. So we each ordered one. It tasted like limeade, except it had a foamy top because they put egg whites in it and whipped it.

It was hot up there on the roof. We couldn't drink the water, so we hadn't had many liquids.

The first pisco sour was small and very tasty. We started our dinners, and before long the waiter came over and asked if we wanted another pisco sour.

"Sure, partner," Scott drawled, "bring us some big ones this time."

So we sat there and drank two or three pisco sours. I thought it was basically limeade.

But when I got up to go to the bathroom, something was wrong. The floor was pointed at about a 45 degree angle toward the swimming pool. I grabbed hold of a nearby pole and hung on until the floor righted itself.

Finally, my head cleared a little, and I went to the bathroom and then back to the table.

"Josh, we're not sl-aying in this hotel any longer," Flash said, looking up at me with a crooked grin on his face. "We're going to go out and she—see—something, see part of Lima. Want to come along?"

I felt sick. "Not me," I said weakly, "I'm going to bed." I'd never been much of a drinker.

A waiter came to the table and asked us if we wanted another drink.

"What's in this?" I asked him.

He grinned. "Is pisco. Made from the grape."

Scott held his head very stiff and blinked, as if trying to keep the waiter in focus. "Kinda strong for wine, isn't it?"

He laughed, obviously enjoying the effect pisco had on the gringos. "Is only 180 proof. That is only 90% alcohol."

We laughed too.

"Only 90%?" Scott asked. "Only 90%? Tastes like limenade."

"I don't think we'd better have any more," I told him.

Scott and Flash started discussing their plans to escape the hotel, and I sat in my chair trying to find the will to get up again and try to find my room.

Then there was a sound of gunfire downstairs, followed by explosions; and the whole building shook.

Chapter Nine

"Wha's at?" Flash tried to get up and almost fell before he got back in his chair.

Scott grabbed his arm to steady him, and we all got up—more slowly this time and staggered downstairs to see what was happening.

Somebody had blown off the front of the hotel. We stood there in the lobby for a while, amidst smoke and dust and rubble. The police had already arrived, and it seemed like people were swarming the place.

Flash leaned against the front desk to keep from falling over. "I think they know we're here."

Scott laughed a little too loudly. "Yeah, we need a lower profile. Somebody's not keeping a lower profile."

I didn't feel so good. "Look, I'm going to bed." I left them and made my way to my room. I was just grateful it was still there.

The next day, a big SUV with armored plating and bulletproof windows arrived to take all twenty of us to the embassy. The site manager had also sent along a couple more cars with machine guns for protection.

Scott laughed as we made our way through the streets of Lima. "I thought we were supposed to be inconspicuous."

Pretty Boy grinned. "What do you mean? Nobody is going to notice us. So we have a few guns sticking out the windows. Who's going to notice?"

At the embassy we went through in-processing. Those who had been hired by the Department of State, like Scott, Flash, me, and a few of the other guys, had diplomatic passports; whereas, the rest of the crew had blue passports. Those of us with diplomatic passports didn't have to go through a security check. The guys with blue passports did because they weren't officials of the embassy of the United States. But we were and were welcome to eat at the cafeteria, to shop at the commissary, even to attend embassy parties. The other guys weren't welcome to anything.

After in-processing, we went to the Carson's office at the airport. He was supposed to introduce us to that part of the world.

Surprisingly, he frowned as we came in, then waved us to chairs, stared hard at us, and said, "You're a bunch of damned S.O.B's. I don't know why you're here. We're doing a pretty good job, and why they sent a whole bunch of new men down here is beyond me."

We just stared back at him. We weren't allowed to tell him that the company he was working for had lost the contract to NATI (National Air Transport Inc.). He was about to be replaced; and one of the guys who had just arrived, Bill, was going to be his replacement.

Those of us who were new were scheduled to go off into the jungle—to see what the jungle operations were like, but the next day the men who had been living there came into town, some of them to the hotel where I was staying. They said the insurance company wouldn't pay any insurance on those who had been killed in the airplane because those men had been killed in a war zone.

"We're not covered out there," one of them said. "So we left the helicopters in the jungle and came back into Lima. If we're killed here, we're covered. And we're not going back until we have insurance."

I got in the habit of going up to the roof for breakfast fairly early in the morning, before anyone else arrived, but the next morning I was late. Pretty Boy was sitting at a table, having a very intense conversation in Spanish with one of the waiters. He nodded at me when I sat down and continued the rapid-fire conversation for another five minutes before the waiter finally took my order and left.

Pretty Boy took a deep breath and shook his head.

"He was just telling me about something that happened this morning. It's unbelievable." He closed his eyes and shook his head again. "I'm not going to laugh when they haul us around in armored cars any more."

"Why? What happened?"

"They blew up a busload of Russian embassy people—embassy personnel and technicians. They were leaving the country, on their way to the airport this morning, and somebody rocketed the bus and threw fire bombs inside."

"Here in Lima?"

He nodded

"Who did it? I mean, I thought the Russians were pretty friendly with the Peruvians."

"They used to be. The Russians have been supporting the Peruvian army and training it for years. Only Peru owes Russia a lot of money, so the Russians decided to pull out."

"But who attacked them? Not the army?"

"Oh, no. The waiter says they don't know who did it. Maybe the *Sendero*. Maybe the Narco Traffickers or the Drones. But they burned everybody on board except for one person. He pulled a panel out on the floor just as the first rocket-propelled grenade started in and went through the hole. Then he hid under the bus as it was blowing up and caught on fire. When it got too hot, he rolled out. Everybody else, the driver and the other passengers are dead."

I was stunned and just sat there, trying to comprehend the thinking of the people who had committed that act. "That's crazy. They were leaving the country. How were they a threat to anyone?"

Pretty Boy sighed. "I know it's crazy. There's lots of craziness in this part of the world. Maybe you get used to it after a while. I don't know. I never have."

I'd heard that the US Marines, the embassy guard, were constantly coming under attack, but this was the first time I'd heard about a massive attack on civilians in Lima. The marines had been bombed and rocketed several nights in a row with considerable loss of life and several injuries.

So Lima was actually a war zone too.

Almost everywhere we went there was trouble with thieves. We were warned that we should go out in groups, for our own protection; but once I ignored that warning and came close to paying for it with my life.

Chapter Ten

It happened one evening when I was walking back from Pizza Ria or Pizza Alley, a restaurant that had baked potatoes. Normally the Peruvians fixed Poppa Puree, mashed potatoes in the form of a thick, yucky soup. They had poppas or French fries that were good, but Pizza Ria was the only place I'd found that served baked potatoes. Their potatoes were imported from the US, because, although Peru had 400 varieties of potato, they didn't have a decent one for baking.

The area I was walking in was a well lighted park about 2 brocks from the hotel. It seemed perfectly safe, with a big iron fence around it and streetlights on the exterior and interior lights as well.

I wasn't the least bit alarmed when four people, three men and a woman, approached from the other direction. They came up to me; and one of them said, "Excuse me, do you happen to have the time?"

I learned that night never to let anyone get close to me, because when I raised my arm to tell them the time, two of the men grabbed my arms and slapped me against the fence.

The other man had on zapper gloves—leather gloves that had been filled with lead shot. He hit me in the stomach several times, then in the kidneys, taking my breath away. It was almost like being hit with a blackjack.

I couldn't kick. I couldn't fight. Two large men were holding me down. I passed out; and when I came to, the woman was sitting on my chest.

They'd gone through all my pockets, taken my wallet, taken my glasses. Then they disappeared.

When I got to my feet, I felt woozy and my nose was bleeding. I covered it with a handkerchief and staggered to the street. I was so sore I could hardly walk. I didn't see anyone else until I got to the hotel. One of the guards let me in but didn't seem to pay much attention to me. Probably thought I was drunk.

The Reverend was in the lobby and his mouth dropped open. "What happened to you?"

"Send a medic . . . to my room."

The Reverend helped me to the elevator and rode up with me then took my key and unlocked the door to my room.

"I'm going on up to the roof," he said. "A couple of the guardians were there when I left."

Most of the guardians were former Navy Seal medics. I hadn't seen Antonio since the mission in Nicaragua, but Antonio, the head guardian, came to my room and examined me. By that time my eyes were almost swollen shut, and my nose was twice its normal size. I found out that I had a black eye, a nose that was almost broken, and a couple of broken ribs. Antonio gave me some painkillers and taped up my rib area.

But even with the painkillers, I had trouble going to sleep, not just because I was hurting but because I was so angry.

The first time I was in Peru I'd been attacked and almost killed. The second time I'd been attacked and beaten up.

For three days I lay in bed, healing and resting up. The longer I lay there, the more furious I became. I vowed I was never going to be attacked again. Or be taken advantage of again. And if I was going to fight, I was going to fight to the death. Never again was I going to end up lying on the ground as a victim of somebody else's greed.

I knew how to fight. The problem was that every other good soldier in the world had the same kind of military training I'd had. They knew how to counter all of the attack moves I'd been taught.

The Department of State taught us some additional hand-to-hand combat, but that too was just like military training. Everybody knew how to fend against it.

I'd lost two battles in a row because I'd been surprised and out-manned and obviously didn't have the necessary skills to survive.

So I lay there in bed and asked myself, "What do I know that is different from my military training?" Two experiences came to mind.

My first job out of the military was as a police patrolman assigned to permanent night duty while I went to college.

One night Duncan, a black policeman, was backing me up; and we arrested a guy who wanted to fight. Duncan slapped the guy across the back of the head with his open hand, and it sounded like a big firecracker going off. Like a gun cracking. The guy's eyes bugged out, and his knees went weak.

"How do you get that much force with such a simple blow?" I asked, and Duncan just laughed.

A few nights later when dealing with a drunk, I tried slapping the man across the back of the head with my open hand, instead of using my night stick or a slapper. But it hurt. A human skull is very hard. All I did was rupture every blood vessel in my fingers. All it did to the drunk was make him madder.

When I took the guy into the station, Duncan happened to be there and saw my hand with the fingers swollen up like giant pickles and starting to turn purple.

"What did you do?"

"I tried to use your open hand slap."

Duncan grimaced and shook his head. "Well, you did it wrong. You aren't supposed to use your fingers, use the heel of your hand."

The department had a big punching bag, and a few days later Duncan and a couple of his buddies showed me how to use the heel of my hand on the punching bag. Using the heel didn't hurt your hand. You could knock a man down with that open hand slap. If you hit him in the face, you could break his nose or his chin. And you could definitely get his attention by hitting him in the back of the head. It took all the starch out of the guy because it's like being up against a world-class, heavy-weight prize fighter when his fist hits the opponent and you hear that loud pop and watch the other person crumble. That's what an open-hand slap will do.

In Alaska I'd learned what almost every Eskimo learned—the one-foot, high kick. While standing flat-footed, an Eskimo can kick up and hit you square in the face. If they use the bounce step, they can kick well above your head. It's one of the Eskimo games.

Another of their games is the two-foot high kick. Standing flat-footed, they can kick up and get both feet well above their heads and manage to do it without falling on their backsides when their feet come down.

I had toyed with those moves; so as soon as I mended, I started practicing them again. I hung a leather pouch head high and tried kicking it. When I first started, I fell down; but soon I got so I could kick with the right foot, then the left, and finally with both feet.

Then later, every time I had time off, I went to Dojo, a karate center. The instructor had perfect English with a Scottish brogue. He taught me to do a better leg sweep and to go for the opponent's knees or his foot or solar plexus. The object was to get that person down on the ground.

I purposely learned a lot of different types of moves and also learned not to pull my hits.

Typically you always stop just before you hit someone so you don't hurt him. But I was practicing to do all the damage I could. To get the opponent on the ground immediately. Then to get away as quickly as I could. And I was using some techniques that nobody else had ever seen.

Lima was definitely a war zone, only not officially a war zone. I became very defensive and never let anybody get behind me. If I walked where there were glass windows, I positioned myself so I could see who was following me. I never again went anywhere without other people, unless I was well armed. That brought up another problem.

Although Lima was a war zone, the ambassador who was in place when we arrived told us that we were not to carry any weapons. That made no sense. We were targets in a hostile environment but were not allowed to carry guns. After my experience with the thieves, I was anxious to get hold of a weapon.

One of the members of our group was nicknamed Polecat. I'd met Polecat during my training in Florida and wondered how he'd come by the nickname, because he was fastidious about taking showers and using deodorant. He'd been recalled to the states because the State Department found out he was living with his wife in Peru. We were not allowed to have wives or girlfriends there.

However, Polecat's wife was Peruvian, and her father was a general in the Peruvian army. The general had provided his daughter and son-in-law with a beautiful mansion next to his own mansion.

This particular general had four brothers, and all had risen to the rank of general. Officially they only made about $25,000 a year, but they were living in multimillion dollar homes—marble floors, marble walls, hand-painted portraits by well-known artists, hand-crafted furniture, servants, yard people, chauffeurs—all supposedly on $25,000 a year.

One day Scott and I were complaining that we were sitting targets without weapons, and Polecat told us that he had weapons he'd gotten with his father-in-law's help. He offered to tell the general about our dilemma and came back a few days later with a list of things we were to buy in order to get some weapons.

We had to get hold of typing ribbon and correction fluid. We had to buy some cigarettes, a couple of bottles of good scotch, and a bottle of American bourbon and place all of these "gifts" in boxes with ribbons around them.

A couple of days later the general and Polecat came by the hotel in a chauffeur-driven limousine and took Scott and me to a government building. First we gave a secretary the typing ribbon and correction fluid, and she typed up a form for us. Then to get the necessary signatures for our gun permits, we were introduced to various other officials (so these officials would know we weren't criminals—Polecat's father-in-law said), and we distributed our gifts.

The Head of the National Police signed the permits, which meant that Scott and I had red cards. A red card was a "get out of jail free" card. We were now part of the national police. We could shoot whomever we wanted—no questions asked.

Then we went outside the city near the airport—the worst part of town—to visit an arms dealer. A tall cement wall surrounded his establishment, and it looked very ordinary from the street. The building itself was green stucco with black bars on the windows—or metal latticework that served as bars.

A dark, slender Peruvian met us at the door and ushered us into an elegant waiting area—polished wooden floor, beamed ceiling, black leather couches with a couple of red armchairs added for color.

A big, light-skinned man with a Clark Gable mustache soon came out to meet us and apologized profusely for keeping us waiting. His hair was combed back like Elvis Presley, and his shirt was unbuttoned to reveal a hairy chest and a gold necklace. He wore hand-made shoes and creased pants and looked like a cross between Wayne Newton and a Colombian drug lord.

He ushered the four of us into his office, a big office containing a soft leather couch and chairs, a large mahogany desk, a bar that sat to one side, and French doors that opened onto a plush, green courtyard.

First the servant served coffee, then after coffee our host showed us his wares. The guns lay in closed wooden cases lined with red, green, or blue velvet—cases with little spotlights aimed at each gun. Our host opened one case at a time. He put on white gloves and took out a Smith & Weston .357 Magnum that I was interested in.

"These must be guns that we can register," the general said.

"You won't find any trouble with this gun."

I assumed that meant it had not been stolen—that I would not be arrested when I tried to register it.

The dealer beamed. "This is superb weapon, stainless steel. You don't have to clean. Like new."

"How much is it?"

"Since you are special friend of the general, I give to you for $600."

The general looked horrified. "Too much. You are trying to cheat us."

The dealer's mouth fell open. "What are you saying? This is excellent gun. I pay very much for this gun."

The general eyed the gun thoughtfully. "Maybe $150."

"One hundred and fifty!" The dealer put his hand to his face. "I have a wife and children. How can I make a living if I give my guns away?"

The conversation switched to Spanish and got a little more animated, with the general calling the dealer a thief and the dealer protesting on behalf of his wife and children.

Then the general named another amount that was totally unsatisfactory.

"I have four sons," the dealer appealed to me. "Do you want to see?" He grabbed a photograph off the desk and stuck it in front of me, and I caught a glimpse of four handsome boys standing side by side with dark hair and dark eyes and smiles that revealed white, even teeth. "I pay good money for this gun. How I can feed my boys," he asked the general, "if I don't make a little profit?"

The general took the photograph and seemed to be saying flattering things about the boys in Spanish. They even argued in French for a while, before they finally settled on a price. Then Scott selected a weapon and the argument started all over again.

I bought the Magnum and a Browning shotgun for about $700 total, and Scott bought a couple of guns too. Then the dealer brought out a bottle of Royal Salute for a round of drinks, and we sipped the scotch and smoked Cuban cigars to celebrate the purchases.

I felt a lot better now that I was armed in Lima. But, of course, we could use our new weapons in the jungle as well; and that's exactly where we were a few days later, when we came under fire for the first time.

Chapter Eleven

THE STATE DEPARTMENT had a problem. Their helicopters still sat out in the jungle, guarded by the Peruvian police. The former ex-pats had been in Bolivia when they found out they didn't have insurance. Their helicopters had run out of fuel, and the Bolivian government wouldn't supply them with gas. So the crews abandoned their helicopters in Bolivia and took an airliner back to Lima.

Naturally, it was important to get the helicopters back to Lima too. Those of us with diplomatic passports received a number of perks, like being able to attend embassy parties, but we had another perk as well. We were covered by embassy insurance—even while in the jungle. So we were the obvious ones to go into the jungle and take the helicopters out.

The State Department rented old planes from Los Palmas, a palm farm so large it even had its own army. First those of us with diplomatic passports had to pick up fuel, so we flew one of those planes, a barely pressurized old Electra, a ratty, old thing, to a jungle base in Peru.

The aluminum seats weren't bolted down. They were just strapped down and had a tendency to move across the floor when the plane hit an air pocket, so we all sat on the floor. Some cables ran up and down the line, kind of like the ones in old trolley cars, that people could hang on to if they wanted to hang onto something while the plane bounced through the air. The local people we were hauling out to the jungle, about a hundred of them, stood during the flight.

The roads in that area of Peru were impassable. Communist rebels often set up barricades or dug trenches across them. Then when people tried to get through, they demanded a toll—money, all the goods the natives were bringing through the jungle to sell, a wife or the children. The rebels might let the farmers return to their homes so they could catch them and rob them again later. Or they might just kill them. Sometimes they raped the women and killed them or merely brutalized them and let them go.

So the safest way for the populace to travel to the city was by air. Though I wasn't sure just how safe that was. Overweight, the plane shuddered when it took off; and when it was pressurized, it filled with exhaust fumes.

Before we landed on a little grass strip, nobody said, "Fasten your seatbelts." or "Put your seats in the upright and locked position." In fact, no one even told us when we were landing.

Most of the locals got off first, carrying packages and suitcases from their trip to town, and were met by several hundred people who had come to greet the plane. Local people, of course, made up this crowd, as well as state policemen and members of the Peruvian army and some ex-pats who met us with cargo trucks.

As I walked down the ramp with my duffle bag, I had the eerie feeling that I'd landed in one of the valleys in Cambodia or Vietnam. That's what it looked like, with jungle terrain and high mountains on one side. Some of the locals made their way toward two small buildings at the side of the strip while others greeted friends or loaded old pickups and cars with baggage.

Almost immediately bullets thumped against the side of the plane.

Then a machine gun went off, and the locals scattered in all directions—some of them running to the cover of small buildings at the edge of the strip—some of them getting behind oil drums or the wheels of the plane.

I ducked behind a plane wheel with Flash Gordon right behind me. We dug through our duffle bags to find our weapons and load them.

Soldiers lay on the ground or had taken cover behind barrels and fired in the general direction of the gunfire, but it was hard to tell where the shots were coming from. The enemy was so far away that we heard bullets zing through the air and thump against the plane before we heard their explosions.

Several people had taken refuge at a structure that stood not more than 50 feet away. It was just some poles and a roof that might have served as a ticket booth, but it had sand bags around it.

"I think we'd be safer over there," I told Flash. "And be able to see better."

We holstered our pistols, grabbed up our duffel bags and rifles, and made for the ticket stand. I'd learned not to run for cover. If I'm being shot at or someone is throwing rocks at me, I have a better chance if I walk. Or if I vary my pace a little. So I started at a run then slowed to a walk until I made it to the sand bags.

Scott was there. He grinned as I got down between him and Antonio, the head guardian. "Hey, partner, did you arrange this welcoming committee?"

I just laughed, and we cautiously looked up over the sand bags at the mountain beyond the airstrip.

"See anything?" I asked Scott.

"Not a thing."

"Where are you?" Antonio yelled into a hand-held radio. "Get out here in a hurry. We're under fire."

I dug my binoculars out of my duffle bag and searched the terrain with them until I saw movement. "There they are. Along the ridge."

Antonio grabbed the binoculars and searched the ridge then spoke into the radio again. "They're along the ridge on the mountain—firing down on us."

"Helicopters?" I asked Antonio.

"Yeah, they're coming in. They're about 2 to 3 minutes away. They were supposed to be here when we arrived."

Soon we heard the drone of helicopters—three of them. The first one made a pass, exchanging fire with the people on the ridge followed by the second and the third helicopters. Then the first helicopter made a high, tight pass and fired at the ridge again. But by that time the enemy had disappeared.

Surprisingly no one at the landing strip had been killed or injured. I inspected the plane and determined that it had not sustained any major damage. So I found some aluminum cans and patched it as the others fueled the plane using a hand pump. Then we loaded fifty 55-gallon drums of fuel on board so we could stop every few miles and refuel the plane.

After we took off, we flew around the combat zone to an airport in Bolivia that had an elevation of 14,000 feet, the plane shuddering again as we took to the sky. There we refueled the drums, loaded them and continued flying. It took us three days to get those helicopters back to Lima.

OUR HOTEL IN Lima was still in shambles. No electricity. No running water. No front on the hotel. Armed guards were posted around the exterior to protect the Americans inside. So we were moved to another hotel about 5 blocks away, the Hostel Miraflores, and we took over the entire hotel.

Our location was supposed to be secret; but when we told the taxicab drivers to take us to the Hostel Miraflores, they'd say, "No, no, no. That's DEA. That's DEA." Then they'd let us off somewhere down the street, and we'd walk the last two or three blocks. Every taxi driver in town knew we were there.

One day Scott and I were sitting at a table in the hotel restaurant and bar when a small, thin man wearing a dark mustache and an oversized trench coat took a seat on a nearby barstool. As soon as he got his beer, he turned to us and smiled broadly.

"This is very nice hotel," he said, sporting a thick European accent. "You stay here long?"

"No, not too long," Scott replied.

That was all the encouragement the little man needed. He picked up his beer and came to our table, set it down, and held out his hand.

"Tairov Ivanovich Merezhkovsky."

We introduced ourselves and Tairov Ivanovich Merezhkovsky joined us.

"I hope you do not mind I sit. I like talk English. I need practice English."

"Not at all," I said, amused. Our new friend seemed just a little too friendly and looked like a character from a bad 40's spy movie, with his mustache and trench coat.

"That's some handle you've got there," Scott said.

"Hannel?"

"Handle. Your name. It's kind of a long name. How about 'Ivan'? Mind if we call you 'Ivan'?"

"Oh, yes." He beamed at us.

"What are you doing in Peru?" I asked.

"I work at Chrysler Company."

"Are you Russian?"

"Oh, no, no. I from Ukraine."

The waiter brought Scott and me a couple of sandwiches; and Ivan sipped his beer, watching us and smiling every time we glanced his way.

"What you doing here?" he asked us as soon as the waiter had left. "Where you work?"

We told him we worked for an oil company and made up some nonsense about the company and the work we were doing. Ivan listened intently but really came to attention when other members of our group, including some of the guardians entered the bar.

"Who these people? Who all these people?"

Ivan, it seemed, was a very curious fellow.

After that Ivan showed up in the hotel bar and restaurant on a regular basis and tried to get buddy-buddy with us. We pegged him as a KGB agent because he was always asking questions and because no one at the Chrysler Company in Lima had ever heard of him.

But we had a lot of free time on our hands then, so we said, "Don't ask so many questions, Ivan. Find us some girlfriends. Show us the sights of Lima."

His eyes lighted up at that because he thought he might get us to talk. So he hired a black taxi to take us around town.

The black taxicabs were big, old Lincolns, Fords, and Mercurys and were almost like limousines. The State Department told us to use black cabs because they were supposed to be safe. But they charged U.S. prices with a five-dollar minimum, in a country where one American dollar would buy a million Peruvian dollars. Most of us started adapting and going to cheaper cabs.

But Ivan hired a black cab and took us to the gold museum and a few other tourist attractions. He was a pretty good guide.

One night Ivan took Flash, Irish, and me to see a movie. Irish was actually a portly man from Arkansas. He had the nickname "Irish" because he claimed Irish ancestry and, like many Irishmen, liked the bottle—a little too much. The main reason Flash and I took him with us that night was to keep him away from the bar.

The night before some of us had been coming back to the hotel in a taxi when we saw a man crawling down the sidewalk on all fours. It was Irish. He was too drunk to walk. We loaded him into our cab, took him to the hotel, and practically carried him to his room. Amazingly, he still had his billfold and watch.

So that night we convinced him to go with us to the movies. He said he felt like hell but agreed to come; otherwise he would have probably ended up on all fours again.

The movie wasn't very expensive, but we had to have a reservation and were escorted to seats in one of the plush, velvet-covered opera boxes that lined the sides of the auditorium. It was an impressive movie theatre--like the theatres in America used to be— with ornate molding, gilded in gold or silver, decorating the ceiling and walls.

Luckily Ivan had made reservations because, although the auditorium must have seated 2,000 or 3,000 people, almost every seat was filled. Before long a waitress came around to get our orders for popcorn and cokes. The two "I's" decided to get meals. Irish ordered a hot dog, and Ivan ordered a steak.

"People very friendly in movie theatre," Ivan told us. "They treat you like king. No shoving. No pushing. No one picks the pockets. I feel very safe here."

So we sat back in our cushioned seats and watched *The Fly*, a Hollywood remake of the classic Vincent Price movie. It was in English with Spanish subtitles.

About a month and a half later the American ambassador was sent out of the country; Carson, the site manager, was replaced; and Underdog and some of the other guardians I'd met before suddenly reappeared. They'd been living in apartments in the area, blending in with the local people.

We were instructed to do the same, to find apartments and hire maids or houseboys to take care of them when we weren't there. In the jungle and in town we were to wear jeans, baseball caps, and cowboy boots instead of military clothing.

I took over the apartment of one of the men who was leaving Peru.

Toni, a maid, who lived in the maid's quarters, came with the apartment. Only about 4'9" or 4'10," Toni was a remarkable maid and became a remarkable friend. She was a cleaning fool—for everything she could reach. The things above her head never got cleaned.

I bought a radio and a color TV for the apartment and for Toni. I also bought a vacuum cleaner that had attachments to help her reach dust and cobwebs above her head.

But she never used it, so I demonstrated it for her one day, showing her how efficient it was. She shook her head vigorously. She didn't speak English and I knew very little Spanish, but her meaning was clear.

She had no use for the "sucadora." It was noisy. It had electricity. It might be dangerous.

One day when I took a clean pair of jeans out of the drawer, I found a hole in them. When I showed her the hole and asked her what had happened to my jeans, she said something that I couldn't understand and finally found a big bar of lye soap in the cabinet and a scrub brush and pantomimed scrubbing the jeans that I assumed must have had spots on them.

"Why didn't you use the washing machine?" I asked.

Finally she made me understand that she did not know how to use the washing machine and dryer, that she'd been washing my clothes using the soap and the brush and then taking them up on the roof and hanging them on a clothesline to dry. I'd wondered why they were always so rough and stiff.

That's when I taught her how to use the washing machine and dryer and bought American commissary soap and fabric softeners. She thought using the washing machine and dryer were great, as was an electric mixer a friend brought from the states.

But there was another item, other than the vacuum cleaner, that Toni would not use—the dishwasher. She washed all the dishes in the sink and used cold water because she believed hot water was bad for her skin—a common belief in that part of the world. But when she opened the refrigerator or freezer, she would always take the scarf she had around her neck and put it over her nose and mouth, because they contained cold air. This cold air, she said, would make her sick. So cold water was good, but cold air was not.

She did most of the shopping, and I came to trust her enough to leave money there for her to use. When she bought things, she kept the receipts and showed them to me. The only thing I never let her pay was the telephone bill. I made a lot of phone calls the month I'd moved in because Deborah was keeping me posted on our son's medical progress. He seemed to be doing much better. His seizures were less frequent and less severe. They had even begun cutting back on the medication he was taking.

She also told me something interesting. My grandparents' old farm had gone on the market, and I wanted to buy it.

Anyhow, my phone bill that month alone was as much as Toni made in a year.

The going rate for a full time, live-in maid was $40 a month. I soon raised her salary to $70 and finally to $100 a month. I had the money, and it didn't mean that much to me.

Toni became very loyal.

I'd always believed that if you treat people well and pay them well, they become loyal. That's what I had to have—someone I could trust.

Since I usually spent two weeks in the jungle and two weeks in Lima, she took care of the apartment and protected it while I was gone—except on the weekends, which she spent with her parents. She did most of the shopping and enabled me to blend in with the local residences.

As part of this "blending-in" process, the new company we were working for told us to paint our aircraft and get rid of the military markings. They brought in new aircraft, like the C123, which is the granddaddy of the C130. In fact, they brought in some of the very aircraft that had been used in Vietnam.

We even got Patches, a famous C123, so called because it had been shot up more than any other plane of its kind in Vietnam but had made it home every time. Patches was a good luck plane because, though it had hundreds and hundreds of bullet holes in it, nobody on board had ever been killed—injured, but not killed.

Those of us who didn't know Spanish took Spanish lessons, and we were all given more formalized training and had to qualify with pistols and rifles. Finally an insurance program was in place, so we were ready to start moving back into the area where the *Sendero Luminoso* and Narco Traffickers and some other bad guys had their headquarters. Our job was to search for and destroy all the cocaine or "coca" we could find.

Part Four: Eradicating Cocaine

Chapter Twelve

The Santa Lucia Base and Surrounding Jungle

OPERATION SNOWCAP WAS put in place by the DEA and the Department of State in 1987 to disrupt the growing, processing, and transportation of cocaine in several foreign countries, including Peru. My job was to maintain the aircraft, the helicopters and airplanes, and participate in missions to eradicate cocaine.

The best way to eradicate cocaine is to find and destroy coca leaves where they are being processed. Farmers pick the leaves and then dry them in areas around the huts. Then they bag them and take them to pozos where there are large pits lined with clay or plastic and put the leaves in chemicals to extract the narcotic properties. Young men and women get in the pits and step on the leaves to get them completely soaked, kind of like the people who stomp on grapes to make wine.

These men and women are easy to identify because their ankles, feet, and legs are always blistered from the chemicals. Even when the wounds healed, they have scars all over their ankles. So it is easy to tell who has been working in the pozos.

Then they strain the leaves out of the mixture, dry it, and bag it or form it into bricks and wrap the bricks with plastic so they can be shipped to the US or to Colombia for the final step in the refining process. Because of the chemicals used, these bags and bricks are highly inflammable. Thus the easiest way to get rid of the cocaine is to burn it.

The usual procedure was for us to fly to a pozo in helicopters and fire machine guns into the air to scare the rock throwers away so we could land. The DEA was not allowed to use force, except in self-defense. So we would hurriedly confiscate and burn all the bricks or bags of coca we could find, while cocaine traffickers and their friends threw rocks at us. As long as they only threw rocks, we couldn't fight back.

The Peruvian police went with us to provide protection, but once when they were supposed to be looking for Narco Traffickers and *Sendero* in a village, they came back to the helicopters carrying musical instruments, radios and TV's that they had stolen at gunpoint.

Polecat was in charge that day, and his face turned purplish red when he saw them. "None of that is going to come aboard my helicopter," he yelled. "We're here to do a job, and the job is to deal with the *Sendero*. Our job is not to steal from the local people."

A Peruvian captain pulled a gun. "We're going to bring our stuff with us."

Polecat pulled a .25 out of his shoulder holster. As soon as I saw Polecat pull his weapon, I drew my .357 magnum, and the first officer drew his weapon.

"You don't bring stolen stuff on my helicopter period," Polecat said. Then he got on the radio and called the other helicopters. "Don't let these people bring stolen goods on board. If any of these people try to put stuff on the helicopters, we're going to leave them."

"We're going to leave you here in bad boy country," he told the captain, "or you're going to leave that merchandise here. We're not going to steal."

The captain finally put his rifle down, maybe because Polecat's father-in-law was a general in the Peruvian army. He had some political thump. Not only that, they all knew Polecat would shoot when he got all irritated and turned purple-red, like he always did. He was ready to do battle.

They laid the merchandise down, and Polecat made them unload their weapons before they got on board.

We often wondered why we didn't have the Sinchis working with us, instead of the National Police. The Sindhis were the Peruvian Special Forces, well-trained, good soldiers. Our purpose in being in that part of the world was to make the people feel happier and safer, not more afraid. The police were often part of the problem.

We were supposed to train the Peruvian police so they could fly.

"This is stupid," Polecat said at one of our meetings. "If we train them to fly, they're going to become Narco Traffickers themselves."

"It's already happened," Scott said, and everyone looked at him in surprise. "When I was getting ready to go to Lima for R&R a couple of weeks ago, I got a shopping list from Ricardo for items that cost hundreds of dollars. He paid me with five crisp hundred dollar bills."

Ricardo was one of our best Peruvian pilots. New hundred dollar bills were narco money. He was only making $215 a month to be in the Peruvian military as a captain. A general only made $250 a month. But they lived in multi-million dollar houses and drove chauffeured cars.

One of the ways to rise to the top in that part of the world was to join the military and get as much graft and money and power as you could accumulate. That's what these young men were doing.

WE BURNED THE bricks or bags of coca in place—just threw gasoline on them and burned them to the ground. We knew we were doing some good because less coca was going out of Peru. At first we were only catching maybe 20% of it. When we burned it in place, we were capturing 50% of the coca that was being produced. Prices for cocaine in the US and Europe went up dramatically.

A few months later, the government changed the rules. The DEA was no longer allowed to burn the coca in place. We had to load it up and transport it to Lima and give it to the Peruvian government.

We found this new rule strange, so we put tracking devices on the coca and found that the ministers in Peru were going to the warehouses and shipping it straight to the United States. We tracked one bag all the way in to Miami and another to New York City.

So we went back to burning the coca in place and got a major reprimand—just because we were destroying the coca before somebody could make a profit off of it.

We were ordered to go back to sending it to Lima.

AFTER A WHILE our missions became routine.

About that time Ho, a Hawaiian who was one of our mechanics, decided to throw a luau. "Don Ho" was his nickname—shortened to Ho—from the Hawaiian singer, which was misleading because he couldn't carry a tune.

He wanted a wild pig, but we didn't have time to go pig hunting. So he finally bought one, put it in a pen, and fed it a special mixture of rice and corn and rum. It seemed like every time I needed him, he was taking care of his pig.

But we had begun to fall into a routine. We usually experienced little or no resistance on our forages into the jungle. Maybe that's one reason we were caught completely off guard twice, and both events occurred just a few months after I'd arrived.

THE FIRST EVENT occurred one day when we went out with four helicopters. We carried some DEA and a full contingent of National Police to an area about an hour and a half from our base. It was kind of a remote area with a big open field, and we suspected a pozo was located nearby.

I was the first officer and sat in the door taking pictures of the Landing Zone.

All of a sudden, "Boom!"

There was a big explosion smack dab in front of the helicopter followed by another explosion almost immediately under the helicopter.

I felt a stinging sensation in my right hip and down my right leg, but didn't think much about it because the feeling soon passed. Besides, about that time a SAM-7, a surface to air missile, came right by the helicopter.

A SAM-7 is very, very accurate if you are at a high altitude, but fortunately we were within 75 feet of the ground.

Immediately the captain went full throttle on the aircraft. We made a hard left banking turn to get out of the zone.

About that time we had another major explosion, and all types of holes started appearing in the helicopter—shrapnel as well as bullets. The enemy had been waiting, and we were caught right in the middle of crossfire.

If they'd been bright, they'd have waited until the helicopters were on the ground before they started shooting all their RPG's (rocket propelled grenades) and automatic weapons. That way they'd have been sure to get all four helicopters.

The captain reconnoitered back up and asked if there were any wounded on board.

Boxer, one of the DEA agents, pointed at me. "You're bleeding everywhere. Your pants are red with blood. Are you hurt?"

"I felt some stinging a few minutes ago. I don't think I'm hurt." But a glance at the side of my right leg showed me that I was, in fact, bleeding.

The first thing we had to do though was secure the Landing Zone. So the helicopters formed up again. None of them was inoperative, although they all had new air conditioning holes in the cabin areas.

This time when the helicopters came in, they came in a full-blown frontal assault, with machine guns firing to silence the area. As soon as a helicopter touched down, the Peruvian Police and DEA went out in formation, and the helicopter went back up immediately, providing covering fire.

Then the next helicopter came in and the next and the next, and the National Police swarmed out.

The helicopter captains adapted a circling combat mode, and the crews started shooting at the edges of the clearing. Every time we saw the flash of a muzzle, we opened fire on that area. We weren't equipped with any type of rockets or mini guns, which would have made us far more effective. We only had 30 caliber machine guns plus rifles and handguns to fire out the door.

After about a 10 or 15 minute full-blown attack on the Landing Zone, the message came over the radio that the area was "secure, secure," so we landed and started looking around.

We didn't find any dead, but we did find some blood trails and the RPG's the enemy had been using as well as some extra rockets. The Narco Traffickers had just dumped them and run.

By the time I got back to the base, I was hurting, so I had the medic check me over and found out I'd been hit by shrapnel in my right leg and buttocks.

"Hey, we have a wounded American. This is a momentous occasion," somebody said, as I was bent over the observation table while the medic extracted little pieces of metal from my rear.

A few minutes later several people came in the room, and Irish had a camera. "Here we have the first American wounded on this particular trip," he said, and everybody laughed and made remarks about how bad the injury was.

A few nights later right before they showed the weekly movie, somebody stuck in the film of me bent over the table and everybody talking about how badly I had been wounded and laughing their heads off.

Meanwhile, Don Ho was still preparing for his luau. Near the base he found some old lava beds and had some of the workers go out there and chop up some of the soft, black rocks. Then they brought back several bags of lava, dug a large pit, for the fire. He planned to wrap the pig in palm leaves or banana leaves on a Saturday morning and let it cook all day and all night to be ready for the next day. He sent the local people out to find baking bananas, rice, yucca roots, apples and a couple of pineapples.

During this time we were caught off guard again.

Chapter Thirteen

We'd had a briefing right after breakfast and were to go to a suspected pozo about 75 kilometers from Santa Lucia. The aerial photographs showed a small encampment with very little protection around it. It looked like the usual pozo, where some of the locals had been taking coca leaves and drying them, getting them ready to process. Near the encampment was a river and along the river was a gravel bar where we could land the helicopters and defend them.

We took two helicopters. Aboard each were a pilot, a first officer or crew chief, two Peruvian gunners, six Peruvian policemen, and four DEA agents. We usually took a medic, and that particular morning Donnie, a Special Forces Medic, was aboard our helicopter.

The sky that morning was clear blue with a few wispy clouds forming off to the east as heat started to rise up off the jungle. A beautiful day.

In less than an hour we were at the location. We made our usual quiet approach—a long, slow straight-in approach across the far side of the valley to muffle the sound of the main rotor blades until we got to the gravel bars along the river.

As soon as we landed, the DEA agents and National Police got off and climbed a hill at the bank of the river and headed through the jungle toward the encampment. Donnie trailed along behind them. He was a Sergeant Major, a former Viet Nam medic. Every time he went to a village, he checked around to see if anyone needed medical care.

The helicopter crews (I was part of one crew) and the two Peruvian gunners stayed with the helicopters to protect them.

After about twenty-five minutes I saw someone running to the helicopter. It was Donnie. Something was wrong.

"It's not just a pozo," he said. "It's a laboratory set up by the Colombians. There are Colombians there, and they've captured the National Police and the DEA. We've got to save them before they're butchered out."

I grabbed my rifle, took off my helmet and ceramic bullet-proof vest and put on my flight jacket and boonie hat. All the time I was wondering how we were going to rescue the others. There were only nine of us, counting Donnie. We'd be vastly outnumbered.

"We go back to the encampment as quickly as possible and surround it," Donnie told us. "I want the pilots and first officers to be my attack. I want the Peruvian officers to stand at their backs to make sure nobody comes up behind them."

We raced up the hill and through the jungle to the encampment and quickly, quietly surrounded it, getting as close as possible.

I could see the Americans standing with their hands tied behind their backs. Three of the Peruvian officers were down on their knees. About a seventy people stood in an open area before a hut. They had just cut off the ear of the senior Peruvian Captain because they'd asked him a question and did not get the answer they wanted.

They were having a great time, laughing and saying, "Mucho oro. Total, total, total." Which meant there would be much money for everybody because the Colombians would pay the people $50,000 for every one of the DEA agents they killed that day.

Their leader was slightly taller than most of the people there and had a Colombian accent. "You don't get any money for the Peruvians," he told them in Spanish. "That is part of your job. But there are eight Americans. You are going to get more money than you'd see in a lifetime."

The crowd laughed and cheered. Several in that crowd were *Sendero* leaders because they were wearing the *Sendero* insignia on their shirts.

"Yes, we will enjoy the killing today," one of *Sendero* yelled.

Donnie had told the pilots and first officers to go around the camp and get down behind something for protection. Then we were each to sight in on a person, one of the leaders if we could.

"When I give a whistle," he'd said, "count three seconds, and we'll all fire at once. I want five people to go down when I fire my weapon." The Peruvian officers were just to protect our backs in case someone got behind us.

As soon as I got in position, I targeted a Colombian.

The Narco Traffickers started kicking their prisoners, and one of Colombians took a hand grenade and placed it on the top of a DEA agent's head. He pointed out that they could make a big bang. Except, he said, it would be better to keep the head for the money instead of blowing it off with a hand grenade. They all laughed.

Then I heard the whistle. I counted one thousand one, one thousand two . . . We'd all picked different targets and all fired at the same time.

Boom! Five people including the leader went down.

Donnie screamed out, "*Manos arriba*! That means "hands up."

And "*Armas bajo*!" That means "put your weapons down."

Instead several people started twirling around. "Now!" Donnie yelled.

We fired again and five more people went down.

Now there had been two volleys coming from five different directions, and there were people on the ground wounded or dying.

The Colombian leader started to stand up, and Donnie screamed at him in Spanish, "*Armas bajo! Armas bajo! Ahora!*" or "Put your rifle down! Now."

The man lifted his weapon, and Donnie fired again, knocking him down, purposely shooting him in the shoulder area so he would drop his rifle; and he fell to the ground.

At that point several of the other people started to move around very quickly

"Again!" Donnie yelled.

And we fired again.

All we had to do was pick out one target and fire. The Narco Traffickers and *Sendero* couldn't tell where we were shooting from because shots were coming from every direction. They were confused. Fifteen or sixteen of their people had been wounded or killed.

That's when they started putting their hands up.

Donnie did not come out of the jungle. He told one of the Peruvians to cut the bonds on the hands of one of the DEA Agents.

"If you do anything else," he said, very clearly in Spanish, "you're dead." The words he used were "*carnie morto*" or "dead meat."

Donnie had a very strong voice; and since he was a Sergeant Major, he was used to giving commands. His voice came bellowing across that jungle.

As soon as they got the first agent's hands loose, that agent immediately cut the other people loose; and they retrieved their weapons. The man who'd cut off the captain's ear was one of those shot. The captain was furious and started yelling at him and kicking him, but Donnie ran in and stopped him.

"We don't have time for that!"

So the battle was won very quickly. The Peruvian Captain had lost his ear and a couple of the Peruvian police had lost fingers. But if we had arrived a few minutes later, they'd have had people slaughtered everywhere—heads chopped off, hands chopped off.

Almost as important as saving the DEA agents and Peruvian Policemen was the fact that we'd captured three Colombians who had come in from Metolene and built a working lab where they could turn the coca into one-to-one and finally refine it into the pure stuff. Then they'd put it in kilo bags and send it from Colombia to the rest of the world for sale.

As soon as we'd disarmed everybody, the DEA and Peruvian Police cuffed them while those of us who were part of the helicopter crews stayed in the jungle providing covering fire. If anybody moved, the people were warned, we would fire again. But as soon as the DEA and Peruvian Police had their weapons again, we relaxed.

Donnie immediately went around and checked each of the people. Those who were wounded, he treated.

Some of the *Sendero* officers and Colombians were dead. Those who were not received first aid. Then the Peruvian Police handcuffed them and took them to the helicopters. The police peeled off the prisoners' clothes to make sure they didn't have guns, hand grenades or knives, and put them in body bags. They were bleeding, and blood is very corrosive to a helicopter. Besides the body bags immobilized them until they could be taken back to Santa Lucia and then on to Lima for further interrogation.

As we went through the camp, we found generators and electric lights inside the huts and a line of electric lights lying along a grass airstrip in a big, open field not far from that location so they could make night take-offs and landings in the middle of the Peruvian jungle. A very sophisticated setup.

We found documentation on the *Sendero Luminoso* as well as the Narco Traffickers—telephone numbers, addresses, and flight schedules. This was the first indication we had that the two groups were beginning to work together.

Drop cloths surrounded the huts so when they operated at night the lights wouldn't show up on the photographs the DEA took every night from the satellite.

We blew up the laboratory with plastic explosives. The cocaine, we contaminated with diesel fuel and set on fire. Theoretically we were supposed to bring it in, but we couldn't bring in the people and the cocaine. So we took pictures and burned it on site.

One thing about the incident really bothered me afterwards—the reaction of the *Sendero* and Narco Traffickers.

I mentioned it to Flash and Ho a couple of mornings later while we were sipping coffee after breakfast.

"What's wrong with these people? They know the DEA agents always come in by helicopter. They know we usually land on gravel bars at the river. Yet they weren't alert for our arrival on the scene. It didn't seem to occur to them that the helicopter crews were even in the area."

Ho laughed. "They're just stupid. They don't have any education."

"American Indians didn't have formal education either, but they were very cagey, very alert to potential danger."

"They're not as smart as American Indians."

"They're smart all right." Snake, one of the guardians, walked over to our table. "But they've been using coca most of their lives, that's what's wrong with them." Snake was former Special Forces and had been working with the DEA for a couple of years. He was bald and thin and wiry and usually wore a grin that was mostly a sneer. That's exactly the kind of expression he was wearing now.

I was puzzled. I didn't think the natives had much access to the finished product, to the cocaine. "They just chew the coca leaves. All that does is relax them, right?"

"Haven't you seen those little bags the natives in the jungle carry with them? They contain pot ash. When they mix that with the coca leaves, it releases the THC. That's what makes their teeth brown or black. That's what keeps them working for 12 hours straight. That's what gives them anxiety attacks—just like cocaine. "

"Yes, but cocaine makes you more mentally alert," Flash said. "That's one of the reasons people use it."

Snake shook his head. "That's just the theory. But I've got another theory. I think you just think you're more mentally alert."

"How do you know?" Ho asked. "Have you used it?"

"No, I've never used it, but I've been on a lot of missions. I've seen how these people act. They just do as they're told. They don't think for themselves."

"Their leaders aren't thinking either," I said. "If they'd been thinking, they'd have told everybody to watch for the rest of the gringos. But they didn't. They didn't post guards. They didn't set up ambushes to capture us as we came through the jungle or send men out to capture the helicopters."

Snake shrugged. "I told you, it's the coca and the pot ash. The leaders chew it too. They all chew the leaves every morning because it gives them energy. But it sure doesn't do anything for their minds. Then it begins to destroy their bodies and they die by the time they're forty."

"Yeah, something's wrong with them," I said. "They seemed to forget all about the helicopters."

Flash frowned. "Then why do they say it heightens your mental ability?"

"Have you ever noticed it doing that? Have you ever had a friend or family member on the stuff? Were they any smarter for taking it?"

Flash didn't say anything, and Snake's laughed, a sardonic laugh. "If it heightened mental ability all the people around here would be Einsteins. Instead they usually act like zombies."

Don Ho got up. "I better take care of my pig."

"I think you're getting attached to that pig," Flash said. "We ever going to get to eat it?"

"This Sunday," Ho said, acting offended. "I've already built a fire in the pit. We're going to eat it this Sunday."

Ho left the tent and hadn't been gone more than a minute or two when we heard him yelling bloody murder.

Chapter Fourteen

WE RAN OUTSIDE and saw one of the strangest things we'd ever seen. Ho was jumping up and down waving his arms while his pigpen leaned to one side and moved slowly toward the river. Not only that, it had grown a tail, a long tail.

"He ate my pig!" Ho yelled. "He ate my pig!"

As I got closer, I discovered that the "he" Ho was referring to was a giant anaconda. It had come into camp during the night, worked its way between the slats of the pen, and eaten the pig. But when the snake tried to get out, he couldn't because of the big lump in his body.

So he had ripped the pen loose and was dragging it back to the banks of the river.

Scott and a few of the others had run up by then, and Ho screamed, "Help me get him!"

Five or six of us tried to grab hold of the snake's tail, which was many, many feet long and almost fell down when it pulled us to one side.

About that time a lot of the Peruvians had arrived, thinking they were going to see the pig. But it was no longer a pig. It was a huge snake with a bulge in its belly. They grabbed hold of the snake too and started laughing and yelling because now there was going to be a big time party. They loved anaconda meat.

It finally took about 20 of us to pick up the snake. Ho eventually cut his belly open and out came the pig. He was dead but not digested.

"Hey," Ho said, "all the snake did is tenderize it for us."

So he washed the pig down and wrapped it with leaves, and he and I carried it over to the big fire pit. Scott and I helped him get the coals just right. Then he added the fruit and vegetables and put more banana leaves on top and more coals and then put dirt over the pit and let the food cook all day.

On Sunday the workers put the anaconda over a fire and roasted it. So about the time the Americans were ready to dig into their pit, the Peruvians came over with a big plate of anaconda meat. It was a white meat, a very chewy meat, and really didn't taste that bad. It wasn't like chicken. It wasn't like shrimp.

About 4:30 that Sunday afternoon, we ate the pig. It was soft, juicy, and well done. The fruit and veggies were tender. We shared our food with everyone and even had some left over.

"Too bad it wasn't a wild pig," Ho said later. "It would have had an even better flavor."

The next day I was still stuffed from my Sunday feast. While I worked on a helicopter engine that morning, I was thinking that I probably wouldn't eat much for the next couple of days. I didn't know how right I was. Not because my stomach was still too full though, but because that afternoon something happened that caused me to loose my appetite completely.

BRIGADIER GENERAL ALBERTO Arciniega ran a town just upriver from Santa Lucia, Uchiza, the drug traffickers main base. At one time 90% of all the coca in the entire world grew there. The general charged drug dealers a $15,000 fee to land and load their planes with cocaine. For larger aircraft he doubled the landing fee to $30,000.

Arciniega had his own little army, and sometimes they had conflicts with the *Sendero Luminoso*. So it didn't come as much of a surprise when the DEA received a report that the *Sendero* had murdered a bunch of Arciniega's Peruvian officers.

It seems that a large force of communists had surrounded several hundred Peruvian soldiers, part of General Arciniega's troops.

"If you surrender your officers," the *Sendero* told the enlisted people, "we won't kill you. We'll let you go free."

So the soldiers had a choice. They could fight until every person was dead or give up their officers. They probably didn't have much affection for their officers anyway, because General Arciniega and his henchmen, like the communists, ruled by terror and intimidation. They surrendered their officers, and the *Sendero* let them go.

The communists then bound those officers, knocked them down, and ran over their heads with trucks while they were still alive.

The DEA got a report that National Policemen had been killed and asked us to investigate. We launched three helicopters and found the remains of twelve officers who had been killed the day before.

They were almost jellified because it was hot in the Amazon Basin. I'd brought some after-shave along, and Scott and I put it on our upper lips to mask the smell as we bagged the men, four for each helicopter, and shipped them to Lima for burial.

That experience was bad enough, but what happened next was even worse.

Later that same day I had just finished working on a plane and was gathering my tools when the Reverend came walking by the shop at a fast clip.

"You won't believe what's floating up," he said.

"What?"

"Why don't you go take a look. I'm going to go get some more help."

I hurriedly put my tools in the shed and walked on over to the Huallaga River where one of the tower guards and a couple of other guys were standing and pointing upstream. .

When I got closer to the bank, I spotted what looked like bags floating toward our camp. The light wasn't very good, so at first I thought I was seeing the debris from a boat that had capsized—maybe bags of rice, even cocaine.

But one of the bags had come to shore and lay at the feet of the tower guard and when I got a good look at it, it made my skin crawl. What I was really seeing was a body—minus the head and hands. In fact, there were lots of headless, handless bodies.

Pretty Boy ran to my side. "What is it?"

"Bodies. Maybe twenty or thirty bodies."

Pretty Boy stopped and stared, muttered something in Spanish and shook his head as if to deny what he was seeing. "Bet they came down from Uchiza, from General Arciniega's town. Bet you anything."

Soon some of the other men came up to the river's edge with body bags, and we pulled the torsos from the river and bagged them. Only it became evident there were too many bodies, two or three hundred. We couldn't pull all of them out.

The next day we heard that General Arciniega, enraged because these soldiers had surrendered their officers, had cut off their hands while they were still alive, then beheaded every one of them and thrown their bodies in the river. The local Indians believed they could not enter the after-life without their hands and heads.

Somehow the world news media got word about what had happened and flew in to interview General Arciniega. Some of the other ex-pats and I flew into Uchiza with Diane Sawyer and a camera crew, because it was King's X day while the media was there.

Fierce-looking armed guards met our helicopter, pointing their guns in every direction. Pretty Boy, our pilot and the interpreter that day, told the guards to put their guns away or there'd be trouble; but then the guards saw the cameras and they were all smiles.

As I walked down the street behind the camera crew, I saw bags of coca under every one of the little buildings to protect it from rainwater. All the houses had transformers and TV antennas. I entered a store that sold mopeds and Rolex watches. These villagers were getting rich off the coca trade.

General Arciniega was a small man with a little mustache and carried himself with the arrogance of Hitler. He wore a stiff officer's hat and Russian fatigues adorned with metals and neatly tucked into riding boots. The tip and hilt of the swagger stick he held under his arm were gold. His front teeth were also gold and gleamed in the sunlight.

When Diane Sawyer asked him about the soldiers who had been killed and thrown into the river, he denied that he'd had anything to do with that. He blamed the deaths on the *Sendero*.

I HAD ANOTHER opportunity to visit Uchiza shortly after the media had gone home.

There was another division of Americans based in Peru, and they flew aircraft with great big radar units on top—old 707's or L10-111's. They also had some C130's that were similarly equipped. When they spotted planes on the radar screen flying into Peru from Colombia or out of Peru to Colombia, they told us; and we'd launch our helicopters.

The Peruvian army had come up with some turbal-prop aircraft that were set up as counter-insurgency fighters, which means they could carry some bombs and 50 caliber machine guns. They were built by the Brazilian government and looked much like old P51 Mustangs, except that they had a tricycle landing gear with a PT6 turbal prop on the front.

When we got the message that there was traffic to or from Colombia, the helicopters would go up and these little fighter planes would go up too.

One day we went up after an airplane that was headed for Uchiza, and I was the crew chief on one of the helicopters.

Polecat said, "Hey, you're a pilot. Can you fly this Cessna that's getting ready to land?"

"Sure."

A Cessna 207 is basically a huge aircraft that can haul several tons.

When the pilot started to land, one helicopter swooped in and got right in front of the plane. Another helicopter got right over it. So the pilot had to stop the airplane.

I jumped out of the helicopter, along with some of the DEA agents. They ran over, opened the door, undid the pilot's seat belt, and jerked him out of the airplane.

He'd already been at one base and picked up a load of coca. He was going to pick up another load there at Uchiza. It sat along the side of the field, ready to load. The DEA ran over and started picking up bundles of coca and putting them aboard the helicopters.

I got into the seat of the airplane.

The little fighters flew overhead, making a couple of low passes and firing their 50 caliber machine guns to keep the hundreds of drug traffickers in town from running out to the airport and throwing rocks.

We couldn't shoot them, and those people knew it. If we did, the news media would say we were shooting innocent bystanders who were throwing rocks at us. So to keep the people away, we fired the machine guns—not at the ground—not at the people—but just so the people could hear the rattle of the guns, warning them to stay in their houses.

The helicopter in front of the plane lifted up and moved to the right.

I pushed the throttle forward and took off down the runway. Then I set the cruise control and flew the ten minutes to the base at Santa Lucia and landed.

On board we made a fantastic discovery.

Chapter Fifteen

WE HAD THE plane, which, of course, was worth a lot, and we had the coca we'd loaded into our helicopters. But on board we found a load of coca that the pilot had already picked up, plus $100,000 for the load he was picking up at Uchiza and the $15,000 landing fee—one hundred and fifteen thousand dollars in all.

The Narco Traffickers and the *Sendero Luminoso* put a bounty of $50,000 on the heads of all the Americans, the first time we landed in the jungle. But within days a poster appeared with my picture on it. In fact, posters appeared with pictures of all the pilots of the planes and helicopters who took part in the capture of the airplane that day.

The bounty for our heads on sticks was no longer just $50,000. It was $150,000. Where did they get the pictures? The picture they used was the one on file with the American embassy. Someone at the embassy had burned off a copy or taken my picture out of the file and made the wanted posters.

So there I was, a simple airplane mechanic, with $150,000 on my head.

AFTER CAPTURING THAT first plane, we almost made a game of capturing planes.

We got excited every time a message came in that a plane was headed our way. "Let's go capture a plane," we'd tell each other. "Let's go capture a Narco Trafficker out of Colombia—capture maybe the drugs, maybe the money."

First two fighter planes went up for protective cover with their machine guns. Then the helicopters would come in. We'd put one helicopter over the airplane and one in front of the airplane and basically force it, once it was on the ground, to stop. If the pilot turned sideways, the helicopter could hover so that the 50-caliber machine gun was pointed directly at him, and we'd tell him, "Stop. Land."

A few weeks passed, and we captured several aircraft using that method.

Then one day the pilot played it a little bit smarter.

We spotted an airplane coming in on the radar cover, headed for Uchiza again. But when the pilot saw the fighter planes, he immediately landed and taxied the plane up in front of a tree. Some of the drug traffickers in Uchiza dragged the other airplanes around to form a wagon train barrier. He jumped out and cut the spark plug wires. Then he flattened the tires, locked the door on the airplane and disappeared into the crowd.

So we landed. Because the pilot had disappeared into a crowd of people who were throwing rocks at us, we didn't have long to look at the plane.

But one of the first things I had been taught at Spartan's A&P School in Tulsa was how to pick a lock. Customers make a habit of bringing in an airplane for inspection, then locking the door, and going on vacation. The mechanics could sit there and wait for the customer to come back with the keys or learn how to pick the lock on the airplanes and the lock on ignition. So being a mechanic, I always carried a set of lock picks in my toolbox.

First a DEA agent inspected the plane to make sure the pilot hadn't left a bomb or something to blow up in our faces. Then I picked the lock on the door. Behind the pilot's seat lay a big packet of money. The pilot had forgotten to take the money.

The pilot had fixed it so we couldn't fly the plane out, so I handed the money to the DEA, and we hurried back to the helicopter with rocks coming at us from all directions.

THAT EVENING POLECAT and I sat in the mess tent venting our frustration about not being able to take the plane.

"Well, at least we got the money," I said.

"Yeah, but we hurt them far more when we take the plane. What happens if they keep this up? We may never get another plane."

It suddenly occurred to me that the answer to the problem was very simple. "Why don't we just lift it out?"

He looked surprised. "Do you know how to do that?"

"When I worked in Alaska, we did it all the time. It was the only way to recover planes sometimes."

I fished a piece of paper out of my pocket and drew a crude picture of an airplane. "You put some cargo straps across the wing spar by taking a couple of fairing strips off the airplane." I showed him just where the straps should be placed. "Then you tie three ropes to it at the tie-down points on each wing and on the tail."

Polecat frowned. "Why do you need tie-down ropes?"

"You need big long ropes, 50-60 feet long. When you get ready to bring the airplane in, the down-wash from the helicopter rotor blades will cause the airplane to jump all over the sky. But if you have some big, long ropes on it, people on the ground can grab hold of the ropes before the plane gets in ground effect and guide it in for a safe landing and disconnect it from the helicopter."

Polecat got up from the table. "Well, let's not just sit here. Let's go talk to the base commander."

EARLY SUNDAY MORNING we arrived at Uchiza in two helicopters. The National Police were supposed to meet us with fifty men, but they had not arrived. When they did arrive, there were ten policemen instead of fifty. The plane was still sitting up against the small tree with other planes crowded around it. We couldn't move the plane and couldn't lift it with the tree leaning over it, so one of the men chopped the tree down with a great big bowie knife that looked like something Rambo might have carried.

The inhabitants of Uchiza stood by their homes at one side of the runway and watched while Scott and I and a couple of other men put cargo straps across the wing spar and attached ropes at the tie-down points. Then we helped stabilize the plane by holding onto the ropes while a helicopter came over and latched onto it. We got in the other helicopter just as the first rock throwers arrived.

They seemed shocked that we still got that plane out of there.

SO THAT BECAME standard practice. Everybody started doing it. If the plane had wrecked, we'd airlift it out. If it was damaged or disabled, we'd airlift it out.

Once we got a report that a Narco Trafficker had tried to land at a little grass strip and had hit a tree at the strip, and it had apparently killed him.

We launched the helicopters and, sure enough, found a Cessna 206, a large cargo plane, up against the only tree on the strip. It had taken some talent to hit that tree. The pilot was still in the plane because a tree limb had come through the windshield and impaled him.

After removing the body, we searched the plane and found $150,000 in twenty dollar bills, wrapped in cellophane. Once again we had managed to get the money before it was exchanged for coca.

Since we couldn't identify the pilot, we buried him later that day. He never was identified. He had no papers on him, and his fingerprints didn't show up on any records on file anywhere.

The plane was not badly damaged. The engine was good, the wings and instruments were good. So we airlifted it out the next morning.

Before long we had hijacked or found and airlifted thirty airplanes. The base at Santa Lucia was beginning to look like a huge airplane junkyard.

Some of them we fixed up for the Peruvians, for their flight training. Some of them were sold for parts. Some of them had been stolen and were returned.

SOMETHING FUNNY HAPPENED once though. We got a call that a twin-engine plane had been captured with the helicopters again. The crews that captured it wanted me to come over and fly it back to the base. So as soon as Polecat could get a helicopter started, we headed toward Uchiza; but then a message came over the radio.

"You don't need to come. People were throwing rocks at us. We had to get out of there. Raol and Jesus are on board, holding a pistol to the pilot's head. They're going to make him fly the plane to Santa Lucia and land it." Roal and Jesus were two Peruvian policemen who had flown on several missions with me as gunners.

So as Polecat and I were about halfway to Uchiza, we saw a Shrike Commander come flying back over. That's a twin engine, high wing plane that's very popular with the Narco Traffickers because it carries such a heavy load.

The pilot buzzed the field at Santa Lucia and made one long, low pass like he was going to land. But instead he shoved the throttles forward and went up and "bye-bye," with the policemen on board. When they didn't come back, the DEA figured the policemen had deserted. I couldn't believe that though. Jesus and Raol were good men, very conscientious men.

Later that day they called us from a small airport in the southern part of Bolivia. I went with the crew to pick them up.

They came walking out of a store and met us by the runway, looking a little sheepish.

"What happened on that plane?" Polecat asked them. "We thought you'd accepted a bribe and taken off for an extended vacation."

"Oh, no, no," Raol said, his eyes big. "That guy was very mean."

"He was just a little, bitty guy," Jesus put in and indicated with his hand that the pilot was only about four feet tall.

"He was taller than that," Raol protested.

Jesus shrugged. "Five feet maybe."

"Anyhow, he was very mean."

"He was a skinny, little guy."

"Okay," Raol said, sounding exasperated, "he wasn't very big, but he scared me. Did he scare you?"

Jesus shrugged.

"I say I am going to shoot him," Roal said, "and he don't care. He say, 'How you gonna fly this plane?' Then I really get to worry because I can't fly the plane. Jesus can't fly the plane."

Jesus shook his head.

"He say, 'What stop me from taking you back to Uchiza or Colombia where they cut you into little pieces?' I say, 'This gun say you don't do that.' But he say, 'Tell you what. If you give me the guns, I fly you to Bolivia and you don't die.' So we give him the guns and he bring us here."

Part Five: Rescue Mission

Chapter Sixteen

AT SANTA LUCIA Base about a month later, the Base Commander called everyone over to one of the sheds to see it we could identify an American or European man whose body had been found on a road in Sendero territory. A couple of Peruvian peasants had come to the base and said, "We have found a gringo, dead. He's been tortured." So the commander sent a couple of helicopters out to get him

I was glad I hadn't known the man—probably in his late 30's or early 40's, light brown hair. Not much else was recognizable.

Usually the women are the ones who torture prisoners. They'd poured boiling water over his body, cut his testicles off, fingers off, and pried his eyes out—all while he was alive. He'd died a horrible death.

No one on the base recognized him, so we put him in a body bag and sent him on to Lima.

A few days later we got a message from the embassy that he was a freelance reporter working for the *Miami Herald*. The council and the embassy had told him, "Do not go to the Rio Yialga Valley."

But he hired a local to guide him and got a private airplane to fly into *Sendero* territory. He landed at a remote base and walked into the area on foot with cameras and tape recorders to make an award-winning exposé about the poor communist *Sendero* and the war they were fighting.

They had killed him and taken a picture of him. Because he was a gringo, the Narco Traffickers probably paid $50,000 for his death.

"Why didn't you protect him!" the *Miami Herald* was screaming.

But how could we protect him? We hadn't even known he was coming.

He was an independent reporter who had come to the area without permission and who had died because of his own stupidity. He thought he could tell them he was a reporter and that would protect him. It didn't.

A few weeks later Pretty Boy and I were back in Lima at a British bar called Benchley's when a couple of young men came into the restaurant to have dinner. They looked different from most people. They were obviously

Americans but had on white shirts and ties. We invited them to sit at our table because the place was very crowded that night. They introduced themselves as John and Brent.

"Are you in Peru on business?" Pretty Boy asked them, as soon as they'd ordered.

Brent, a nice looking kid with dark hair and eyes, laughed. "No, we're Mormons."

John, the other young man was a studious-looking kid—short brown hair, thick glasses. He never seemed to smile. "We've come to Peru to bring the word of the Mormon faith to the people of Catholic faith and the old Indian religions."

"Here in Lima?" Pretty Boy asked.

John looked even more serious. "No, we're going to go out to Tingo Maria and La Cheeza where the word of God has never been brought to these heathens."

Pretty Boy, who had been about to take a bite of his cheeseburger, slammed it down on his plate, threw up his hands, and uttered expletives in Spanish.

Maybe it was just the force of Pretty Boy's words or maybe Brent knew Spanish because his face turned red, and he almost dropped his water glass.

I put my fork down, my dinner forgotten. "Do you have permission to go to that part of Peru?"

John glared at me. "We know where we're supposed to go."

"That's the worst possible place you could go to. Not even the Spanish Conquistadors could make an impact on that part of the world. It's bad boy country. That's where the communists and Narco Traffickers are. That's were the Le Drones are. The super corrupt drug traffickers work out of that area."

Brent seemed concerned, but my words hadn't fazed the other kid. "Isn't that precisely why the gospel needs to be preached there? Those are the kinds of people who need what we have to say."

"Yes, if they'd even give you a chance to say anything," I said. "We work in that area. We know what those people are like."

"Believe me," Pretty Boy told them, "if you go out there we'll be bringing your bodies out."

"The Lord will protect us," John said, sounding almost haughty.

We argued with the young men off and on all through dinner, even telling them about the reporter we'd brought out just a few weeks before.

They were definitely upset by the conversation with us but remained resolved to go to La Cheeza and Tingo Maria.

When they'd finished eating, I insisted on buying their dinners.

"Has it occurred to you," Pretty Boy said bitterly as they rose from the table, "that maybe God is trying to tell you, through us, that you should not go there?"

Even John smiled at the idea that God would be speaking to them through Pretty Boy.

"We appreciate your concern," Brent said. "We really do." He waved a hand at us. "Hope we see you again."

Pretty Boy sighed as they went out the door. "Yeah, they're going without weapons, without permission, going into the worst part of Peru—and for what?" He laughed dryly. "We'll see them all right. But we'll only see their corpses."

I felt sick at my stomach. "I hope they have strong faith."

About fifteen days later I had that same feeling in the pit of my stomach when we got word at Santa Lucia that two Americans had been tortured to death and dumped by a road near the base.

Chapter Seventeen

I wondered at the time if the bodies they'd found could possibly be those two young Mormon men.

Unfortunately, they were.

I helped load their disfigured bodies into bags while the troops we'd brought with us stood guard. When we got back to camp, I told the commander that I knew the young men. The embassy sent me their names and addresses, and a few nights later I sat down and wrote a letter to their parents that they had died in the mission of their God even though I had begged them not to go into that part of the world. I didn't tell them how the young men had been tortured.

Perhaps, I was thinking as I sealed the envelope, the death of these two young men would convince the Mormon Church that it was dangerous to allow its missionaries to go to the jungles of Peru.

But only a few months later a couple of our helicopters had to land at the police compound in Tingo Maria because they were having mechanical problems, so Snake, Underdog, and I accompanied by some of the Peruvian policemen, flew to Tingo Maria to take care of the helicopters while the DEA and some of the Peruvians went on a mission. Late that morning, while I was sitting under the belly of a helicopter, Snake came walking over to tell me we'd just received a message from the embassy.

"A message? What kind of message?"

"It seems we have a couple more Mormon missionaries loose in the area."

Feeling that familiar tightness in my stomach, I crawled out. That wasn't exactly the news I wanted to hear right before lunch. "Where are the bodies?"

Snake grinned his ironic grin. "Oh, no bodies. Not yet anyway. But these two guys called their parents and told them they were on their way to Tingo Maria. And someone saw their bicycles—American bikes—in town. One of them is painted red."

Ordinarily the bikes in that part of the world were Chinese or Latin American and were black or dark blue.

"However, a motorist said he saw two gringos being held at gunpoint. They had their hands tied and their eyes covered with a blindfold as they were being dragged away."

I slammed the wrench I held on the ground. Why on earth had their church allowed them to come to this area? I was furious, but I was also puzzled by Snake's report. "Why would the *Sendero* blindfold them? Isn't that unusual?"

"Yeah, it is. Maybe they're going to hold them for ransom or show a video of them and claim that they are DEA and show a public execution. Anyhow, we're the only ex-pats here, so we're elected to find out if there is any truth to this story. Find out if they are still alive."

I stood. I'd lost interest in repairing helicopters. I was sick of seeing people butchered. But we'd have to act quickly. I checked my billfold to make sure I still had some fifty-dollar bills.

"I know one of the merchants pretty well," I said. "I think he might help us."

"Okay. Want me to come along?"

"No, I'd better go alone."

On an earlier trip to Tinglo Maria I had stopped at a small store that, along with the usual inventory of soda pop and ice cream, sold some beautifully crafted fishing poles and nets and baskets and mats. The old man who ran the shop was of Japanese descent, and I'd become friendly with him because I admired his handiwork.

So I went to the shop and pretended to be interested in buying something until another customer left.

On seeing me the owner smiled broadly. "Well, it is good to see you."

"Nice to see you again too. But I came to ask you a question. Have you heard about the two missionaries who were near Tingo Maria when they were abducted by the *Sendero*?"

"Oh, no, no." He shook his head nervously, his eyes wide. "I don't know anything."

I picked up a basket that only cost a few pecos, then pulled out my wallet and took out a fifty dollar bill and gave it to the old man. "This is yours. If you have any information that you can get to me within the next few hours, there will be another fifty dollar bill for you."

I took his basket and left.

About three hours later, at about 11:00 o'clock, I received a message that there was a person at the front of the Police Compound asking for me--the old man. He carried a bag as if making a delivery.

"I'm here to get my other fifty dollar bill."

I opened my billfold and took out the money. "First give me the information."

"I have it on very good knowledge that they are here in Tingo Mario being held in a house over by the river."

I handed him the bill. "I need to know exactly which house they're in. If you can get that exact information, I'll get a third fifty dollars for you."

The old man disappeared. A hundred dollars was basically a third of a year's salary for someone back in the jungle, and I was handing out fifty-dollar bills like they weren't going to end.

Less than an hour later, he came back with a small map he'd drawn to show me exactly which house the young men were in, so I paid him and told him that if the missionaries were at the house, there would be a fourth fifty-dollar bill.

"Will you take us there?'

"No, no," he said quickly, backing away, "I can't do that."

"I don't think we should tell the National Police," Underdog said when I shared the information with him and Snake.

"Well, we have to tell some of them," Snake said. "We aren't allowed to make arrests by ourselves. We've got to take some of the Peruvians with us. I'm pretty sure we can trust Jesus and Raol."

They were the Peruvian gunners who'd tried to hijack the Colombian plane but had been outsmarted by the small, cagey pilot.

So we got a jeep and a truck and drove into town.

First we had to make sure the people we were seeking were at the house. We all wore civilian clothes and carried rifles or pistols, which was not unusual because Tingo Maria was like a wild west town, where people often carried weapons, even automatic weapons. It was dangerous country.

We planned to surround the building very quietly, put plastic explosives on the hinges, and throw stun grenades inside. They make a very loud bang and flash a blinding light. Then we'd break into the house and see if the missionaries were there.

The first thing we saw when we drove by the house was a red bicycle standing beside the front door and next to it an American-made blue bicycle. But what really caught our attention was that red bike.

We parked half a block away, got out of the vehicles, and made our way casually up the street. Snake walked about 20 feet ahead of us, followed by Underdog and me and then the two Peruvians. We chatted with one another and stopped across the street while Snake strolled up to the house and put a glob of plastic explosive hear the top hinge of the front door. Though the house was old, the door looked fairly new and had a window at the top.

Snake then walked around the corner to the back.

A few minutes later Underdog crossed the street and kind of stood against the house, which was not unusual, and very carefully put another glob toward the bottom hinge. When he'd finished, he joined me again; and we smiled and chatted and casually observed the house.

Snake was watching the back of the house; and on a nod from him, Underdog and I walked across the street and knocked quickly on the door.

Then Underdog took out his pistol and smashed the window and threw a concussion grenade inside. Just as it went off, we triggered the detonators that blew the door off. And charged in.

A man just inside had been blinded by the blast. Underdog knocked the pistol out of his hand and knocked him down.

I ran through the smoke to the rooms in the back of the house and searched until I found the two Mormons. They were bound and gagged.

I quickly pulled the blindfold off one of them, jerked the duck tape from his mouth, and removed the rag. "I'm an American."

"Thank God," he said excitedly. "Thank God. An American."

I pulled the blindfold off the other young man and took the gag out of his mouth too.

He mumbled something, but his lips and right cheek were puffy. He could hardly talk.

I cut the bands on their wrists and ankles with my knife.

"Come on. We've got to get out of here."

Snake joined me, and we yanked the two missionaries up and went out the door.

By that time Jesus and Raol were inside and had arrested the three people in the house. Two of them had been knocked down and were almost unconscious because of the stun grenade. The third had been disarmed, cuffed, and quickly dragged to the truck.

As we started across the yard, one of the young men yelled, "My bicycle. I've got to have my bicycle!" He seemed more intent on saving his bicycle than saving his life. So Snake and I went back.

By that time, because of the explosion, people were starting to gather around. We had three prisoners and the two hostages, and were in no position to do battle with the other people. But we got the bicycles and pushed them quickly down the street and threw them in the truck

Then I got in the back of the truck with the two missionaries and Raol and Jesus, and we made haste to the Police Compound on the other side of town.

I asked the missionaries if they were injured, if they'd been tortured.

One of them shook his head. "We're kind of bruised. They hit us and kicked us."

They apparently had not been treated too badly up to that time.

As soon as we got back to the Police Compound, we got on the radio and called the ambassador to tell him we'd rescued the two Americans.

"How did you do that?"

"We blew the door off the house they were in and ran in and got them," I said.

"You blew the door off?" The ambassador sounded alarmed. "That creates a problem. You are not allowed to take offensive military action to rescue two Americans who are not part of the embassy staff."

"You told us to look into this matter," I said, feeling the heat beginning to rise around my collar. "Did you just want us to leave them there?"

"I told you to see if you could locate them!" the ambassador screamed into the radio. "I did not tell you to blow doors off houses. I did not tell you to take military action. You are in violation of a number of rules and regulations. I want to talk to all of you immediately. Get back to Santa Lucia and get on the first available plane, along with the missionaries and the two guardians." And thus ended the conversation.

We were stunned. We'd supposedly just created an international incident.

Chapter Eighteen

WE HADN'T KILLED anybody. We had rescued two people.

"I can't believe these stupid bureaucrats!" Snake said, between gritted teeth.

"We used grenades," he whined, imitating a timid pencil pusher. "Oh, my goodness. We aren't supposed to use plastic explosives to blow a door off"

Underdog laughed. "Fortunately, it was the right door."

Forty-five minutes later a helicopter came by to take us, including the Mormons to Santa Lucia. At the base a Hyper Turbo-Pump Navaho, one of the DEA aircraft was waiting to take us all to Lima. It's a pressurized airplane and makes a faster and more comfortable flight back than a C123, which we usually rode in and which is not pressurized. We were traveling in luxury.

At Lima an armored embassy vehicle waited to take us to the ambassador's office. Then Embassy guard ushered us into his outer office and told us he wanted to see Snake, Underdog, and me immediately, leaving the two missionaries in the outer office.

First he met us at the door and frowned, looking very severe; then he grasped our hands and smiled. "I'm glad you did something good."

He sat down behind his desk and motioned us to chairs. "But you violated rule after rule. So what do I do? Nothing? Or send you out of the country?"

"Yeah, yeah, yeah," we said in chorus. "Send us out of the country."

The ambassador chuckled then punched a button on the intercom. "I'd like to see the missionaries."

When the two young men came in, the ambassador introduced himself and shook their hands.

"You weren't tortured? You were just roughed up some?"

"They hit us a few times," one of them spoke up. He was a clean-cut kid, with dark hair and green eyes, of medium build. His left eye was swollen. Except for that he could have been a movie star.

The other young man had curly blond hair and a gaunt face and frame. His lips were bruised and it looked like he'd been kicked in the side of the face. He'd said very little since the rescue, content to let his friend do most of the talking.

"You know you were very lucky. We sent a couple of Mormon missionaries out of here a few months ago in body bags. They'd been tortured. That's probably what would have happened to you, if these men hadn't found you."

"Yes," the dark-hair kid eyed us soberly, "we're very grateful."

"Are you ready to go back to the states now?"

The young Mormon seemed surprised at the question. "Oh, no. We came to Peru to do missionary work. Our work isn't finished yet."

The ambassador turned to the blond-haired missionary. "Do you agree with that? Do you still want to stay in Peru?"

The blond nodded.

He sent them out of his office and closed the door and turned to us, a look of frustration on his face. "Now what do we do?"

"It's no good trying to reason with them," I said. "I tried to reason with those other two missionaries and got nowhere."

"And they can't stay in Peru," Snake spoke up. "The communists will pick them up again in a heartbeat. They were rescued from the *Sendero*. The *Senderos* are not going to let go of it. Those two guys are marked."

The ambassador started pacing. "I know. The embassy can't protect them. They have no embassy protection whatever. Any suggestions?"

One of the lawyers came in and said that the missionaries had valid passports.

He stopped in mid-stride. "I think I know how to take care of this." He picked up the phone and called the head of immigration for Peru. "The visas that were issued to these two young American missionaries, I want them suspended, revoked today. I want an official letter from you over here as quickly as possible."

When he hung up, the lawyer smiled. "But if they don't have visas, it's illegal for them to be in the country."

"Exactly, and they won't be in the country much longer. It's simple. I'm revoking their visas and their passports. So we have to send them home immediately. A C130 is scheduled to bring supplies in here tonight from Panama. I want the two young men aboard that C130 for the return trip, and I want them under embassy guard."

Embassy guards are basically the embassy police.

"They'll have to stay in the embassy until it's time to go to the airport. Then they'll go in an armored vehicle. I'm sending them home. Period."

The lawyer left and the ambassador turned to us. "We're not leaving them in the country where they're going to be butchered. We've already had the success of keeping them alive. If we put them back on the street, if they show up at Benchley's, somebody's going to capture them again and kill them just to prove a point."

He punched an intercom button. "Send the missionaries back in and send the embassy guard."

The ambassador met them at the door. "These two young men are illegal aliens in Peru," he snapped at the guards.

The missionaries' mouths fell open in disbelief.

"But . . . how is that possible?" the dark-haired one spoke up.

"I just had your visas revoked. And I am now revoking your passports. I've arranged transportation for you. You'll be leaving tonight aboard a C130, transported to Panama, from there to the US. There US marshals will meet you, and you'll be arraigned for being in Peru without a proper visa. You are not coming back to Peru as long as I'm ambassador here."

"But that's not right," the blond spoke up for the first time, "we didn't do anything wrong."

"You ignored all the warnings that everybody gave you," the ambassador said angrily. "You got yourselves captured and almost created an international incident. These men will escort you to a holding cell here in the embassy until we take you to the airport tonight."

After the guards and missionaries had left the room, the ambassador turned and regarded us with a smile. "Gentlemen, what are you drinking?"

"Well, I normally take a Coke," I said and the others laughed.

The ambassador walked over to a small bar at the side of the room. "Sorry, I don't have any cokes, but I have some bourbon. I'm going to pour everybody a shot of bourbon."

"You did very well," the ambassador told us, after we'd dutifully drunk our bourbon and were getting ready to leave. "You did not kill anybody. And this means these missionaries won't be able to travel to Peru or Colombia or any of the other countries around here to do their work. I don't want another American murdered. I don't want to read in the newspapers that another young man—like the reporter and the two other missionaries—have been tortured and killed."

He stopped me as I was going out the door. "By the way, how did you get the information so quickly?"

"I paid for it with fifty dollar bills."

"That was smart thinking."

A few days later the ambassador invited Underdog, Snake, and me to a party at his home. Actually we were not just invited, we were required to attend. We sat at the head table, and he introduced us as men who had done the embassy a very big favor. Nobody explained what the favor had been. But, in fact, the dinner had been given for us in appreciation for what we'd done.

I only had one complaint about that experience. I was never repaid the $200 I'd paid to bribe the old Peruvian shopkeeper because it was not an "embassy expense."

In the meantime, bombings had escalated in Lima, and one of those bombs landed very close to home.

Part Six:
Sendero Rampage

Chapter Nineteen

There weren't any American restaurants in Lima, so Scott and I decided to open one. I put up two thirds of the cash needed to buy a restaurant, and Scott put up the rest. We would take turns running it when we were in town and Scott's girlfriend, a tall, savvy Peruvian, would run it for us when we were both in the jungle. You had to have a Peruvian as a partner, or you couldn't have a business in Peru.

The restaurant we found was near the center of Mira Flores with windows opening onto a courtyard. Across the street stood a large hotel, the Americana, a beautiful glass structure that the Colombians had built as a way to launder money.

The restaurant had to have its own armed guards. Naturally, the guards had to be in uniforms and have business cards. That was the protocol in that part of the world. The permits for their shotguns alone were $1500 each.

We used waitresses rather than waiters, although waiters were the custom in Peru. The waitresses had to be able to speak at least two languages and were not allowed to date customers.

American or Peruvian music played over the speakers, with a live band on Fridays and Saturdays.

One Saturday I was sitting at a table going over the list of supplies when a skinny, old woman in her late 60's with wrinkled, leathery skin, walked up to me.

"I'm Lillian Birch," she said, her voice husky, like she'd smoked too much. "I'm originally from Tennessee. How would you like to increase your menu and go to a breakfast menu?"

I had never given that possibility much thought. "Well, I don't know."

"I'm a breakfast cook, and I cook old fashioned American style food—the best biscuits you've ever tasted."

My mouth watered just thinking about it. I hadn't had a biscuit since I'd been in Peru.

"I make really good red-eye gravy, cream gravy, even brown gravy." Her eyes twinkled and a grin parted the wrinkles on her face. "I make the best pancakes you've ever eaten, and I make some pretty good waffles too if I've got a waffle iron."

"Did you say biscuits?"

She went back to the kitchen and made some biscuits that were two and a half inches high, light and fluffy. Then she whipped up some gravy to put on top of them.

Needless to say, we started opening at 5:30 and added a breakfast menu.

Lillian would go to the market and get plain, old Peruvian pork and put various rubs on it and fix it up to taste like fine ham. She bought jams and recooked them, squeezing in a little lemon and other flavors. The final products tasted like they were homemade.

Once the word got out, company busses lined up on the street outside to let their employees eat breakfast at the *Turberna International* before they went to the airport.

Oddly enough, only one place in Lima sold tortillas, the Mexican embassy, and they only made twelve dozen a day. So we bought and saved shells for a time when the marines came in or some other group and had a taco-eating contest. If the CB's ate 28 tacos, the SF would have to eat 40 tacos. One night they ate more than 100 apiece. At two dollars each, Scott and I made a tidy profit.

In fact, the restaurant was very profitable from the very beginning. But having a restaurant was not without hazards. After all, Lima was a war zone.

ONE FRIDAY NIGHT both Scott and I were in town at the restaurant, when we heard a loud explosion that shook the entire building.

The musicians stopped in mid-song, and even the drunkest patron was suddenly sober.

"That was a bomb," somebody yelled. Then everyone was talking at once and scrambling for the door to go out and see what had happened.

About the time they got out on the street, there was a second larger explosion. Every window in the hotel across the street was blown out and glass came raining down.

So here came the people running back in, some of them cut and bleeding; and the patio was covered with a couple of inches of broken glass—a bloody mess. If they'd stayed in the restaurant, they'd have been fine.

I got the first aid kit, and the telephone started ringing with people calling to see if their friends and family were okay. I finally had to put someone on the phone to take calls and relay information about customers.

Scott and I opened the first aid kit and used the tweezers to pluck glass out of our customers; clean their wounds; stitch them, if necessary; and apply some antibiotic cream, until everyone in the restaurant was patched up.

Scott lived in the same apartment building I did, and we finally closed up and started walking home. But when we got close, we could smell smoke and see debris. Then we came to a barricade across the street. Luckily we had National Police ID's, so we walked on in and were astonished at what we saw.

Chapter Twenty

THE BOMBS HAD hit our neighborhood and gutted our apartment house. Our apartments were gone. The scene looked much like the scene after the bombing of the Murrah Federal Building in Oklahoma City. I was glad Toni, my maid, visited her parents on the weekends.

Soldiers and National Police swarmed the rubble. Although an hour or so had passed since the bombing, there were no ambulances, no first aid people. When the police brought the injured out of the buildings, they sat down amidst the debris holding their bodies, or they lay unconscious on the ground.

Scott and I were pretty good medics, so we went to a *parmacia* or drugstore to get some supplies and beat on the door until the owner, a little man with horn-rimmed glasses and a big nose, opened the door just a slit to peek at us.

I slipped my National Police ID through the opening. "We need some first aid supplies. There are a bunch of people just down the street who need help."

"I heard the bombs. Terrible." he said, as he let us in. "What do you need?"

"Morphine, bandages, dressings, and tourniquets to start with."

"And some lipstick," Scott added. "So we can write "M's" on the foreheads of those we give morphine to."

We gathered up everything we thought we might need, which was just about everything the drugstore had, and loaded it into two shopping carts. Then the druggist presented us with a bill.

"But this is for an emergency—for your neighbors," I said, irritated.

"I can't give my medicine away. How can I feed my wife and family if I--."

"Okay. Okay." I'd heard it all before. I just pulled out my billfold and paid the man.

When we got back to the building, the rescue people still hadn't arrived. We set up a triage and laid the people out on the ground.

If they were dead, we just covered their faces. If they were alive and missing an arm or leg, we applied a tourniquet and gave them morphine and wrote "M" on their foreheads. There were only a hundred or a hundred and fifty people to take care of. There should have been several hundred, but all the rest were dead, including the 20 or 30 doctors who lived directly below me.

People from other apartments houses brought flashlights, candles, and oil lamps, for the Americans to work by. They gave us blankets and helped out in any way they could.

About two and a half hours after the bombings, the emergency vehicles arrived to take the injured to the hospital.

Finally, there was nothing left but the dead and the people trapped in buildings.

Scott and I just stood around for a few minutes, not knowing what to do next. We were covered with blood, mud, and dirt.

"Where do we go now?" Scott asked. "We can't go to our apartments. We can't check in at the Americana."

"Let's go find a cab. Go to the Sheridan down town."

We walked a few blocks to Pizza Alley, a business section of Mira Flores that had been unaffected by the bombing, and caught a taxi and went to the Sheridan Hotel in downtown Lima and told the people at the desk that we needed rooms and clothes and needed to have the clothes we were wearing laundered.

The Sheridan Hotel was our home for the next few days, while we found new apartments and bought new clothes and furnishings.

On the next day after the bombing, we finally found out what had happened.

It seems that the *Sendero* was going to try to rob the bank a couple of blocks from our apartment house. When the guards saw the people coming up in two vans full of explosives with dynamite detonators, they drove them away. So the terrorists pulled down some side streets, lit the fuses on the dynamite and ran. They didn't care who was hurt. They just wanted to cause havoc and chaos. To disrupt the economy, the people.

One night the *Sendero* said they were going to bomb every bank in the city. They drove up to a night depositories, deposited their bombs, and blew the windows out.

They particularly enjoyed blowing up businesses with American names. Once they entered a Kentucky Fried Chicken and told everybody to get out that they were going to blow the place up. And they blew it up. The only person hurt was someone trying to get his car started when the building fell on it. Usually innocent bystanders weren't so lucky.

One night a few months after my apartment was destroyed, the *Sendero* set off 50 bombs in and around Mira Flores. I was sitting at an outdoor restaurant at Pizza Alley. The restaurants in Pizza Alley served very bad pizza; and though they called their pizzas Chicago or New York pizza, they were actually served European style, with olives containing the pits and topped with hard-boiled eggs in their shells.

That night as the bombs went off, the people at Pizza Alley clapped and cheered for every bomb. I stopped counting them after fifty.

With one bomb the *Sendero* tried to blow up the Christmas tree on the main square at Mira Flores. They were so inept that all they did was blow off the ornaments on the bottom branches.

Ambulances and fire trucks screamed down the streets. National Police cars raced by, their sirens and horns blaring.

A lot of innocent people were hurt or killed that night.

A week later I was almost relieved to be back in the jungle. My relief didn't last long though because I had to spend some time at Maza Mari.

Maza Mari means "valley of the snakes." That's where the U.S. Special Forces were training the Sinchis, the Peruvian Special Forces. While I was there, a couple of things happened that brought tears to my eyes for months, because of the cruelty of the *Sendero*.

Chapter Twenty-One

THE VILLAGE OF Maza Mari lay deep in the interior of Peru. Originally a native village, a large number of Swiss and Germans had moved to Maza Mari after the first and second world wars. Erick, one of our Peruvian pilots, had originally come from there.

The village contained a few stores or bodagas that had been painted green, blue, yellow, or red, as was the custom in that part of the world. But the farms and homesteads reminded me of the pictures I'd seen of small Swiss villages, with rock houses, barns, and beautifully manicured fields, surrounded by stone fences. The large dairy herds in the area produced milk, cheese, and ice cream; and the fruit trees produced fruit of every variety.

The whole town had been cut off when the civil war broke out. Bridges and roads had been destroyed or were blocked by the *Sendero*. It was too dangerous for farmers to take their products to market, so most of their crops were lost every year.

I once bought a kilo of oranges for a dollar and found it interesting that the bag to put the fruit in cost me another dollar.

In many ways though the village was very primitive. The women who washed our clothes washed them at the river, beating them on rocks and breaking all the buttons.

I soon got used to having all the buttons on my shirts broken.

The base there had originally been built by the United States as a training camp, when Che Guevaro, Castro's right hand man, was the leader of communist guerrilla movements in Uruguay, Brazil, Paraguay, Argentina, and Bolivia and was creating a great deal of anti-government warfare in those countries. In fact, the troops trained at Maza Mari were the ones who eventually tracked Che Guevaro down and killed him.

A few us were assigned there for temporary duty and joined up with the Special Forces who were training the Sinchis to track terrorists—by going through the jungle quietly, repelling out of helicopters, and making parachute jumps.

The members of Special Forces (SF) make up a unique group of people. To get in you have to be a three stripper or a sergeant. A sergeant major is in charge. They have one colonel and one captain, but everything passes through the sergeant major.

The SF don't shine their boots but are the most professional soldiers in the entire world. They learn multiple languages and cross-train in communications, electronics, and medicine. If one of them gets hurt on a mission, there are ten who can take care of him.

We arrived at twilight and were escorted to our quarters by Roberts, a big, burly man of about 40 with a burr haircut and a blond handlebar mustache. Instead of living in tents, we'd be living in regular buildings with kitchens and bathrooms that contained showers and hot water. We were amazed at the luxury.

The electricity in our units hadn't been turned on, but Roberts said the generator was near my room, to just go back and hit the electric starter. But when I went back there, I saw a man lying on the ground, breathing hard. This man had one unique feature—a bullet hole right between his eyes.

I went back to the sergeant major's office.

"Is there supposed to be a wounded man lying by the generator?"

Startled, he looked up from his paperwork. "No."

"Do you know anything about him?"

"Roberts!" the sergeant major yelled, and Roberts and a couple of other guys came to the door of his office as he got up from his chair. "Show us."

They followed me to the generator. When they saw the wounded man, the sergeant major called the base commander. It turned out that this man had been one of the terrorists they were going to bury later that day. They'd shot him, but he was still alive. So they picked him up and dragged him out. Then I heard a couple of shots. That was my first day at Maza Mari.

I soon learned that the SF liked to eat well and live well. We each pitched in a certain number of dollars every now and then to buy a cow or pig to butcher for fresh meat. We also had fresh fruit and vegetables. At the other camps we had eaten rice or fishy rice. But now we even had showers with hot water. We had videos to watch. It was like being on a picnic to be there.

A long grass runway lay at the back of the base, and my job was to keep the helicopters in running order. Late one afternoon when I was on the field checking the timing on a helicopter, some native people came walking toward the camp, pushing a shopping cart. The guard stopped them and called for a medic. These people were hurt.

I grabbed my first aid kit and, along with some other medics, went to the front gate where about dozen people of Spanish and Indian descent waited. A couple of the men had bullet wounds. Some of the women had machete and bullet wounds. In the shopping basket sat a little girl about four years old, with the biggest, blackest eyes I'd ever seen. A bullet from an AK47 had gone through her back. It didn't hit the spine, but the wound was badly infected.

The base commander called a Peruvian interpreter out because the people mainly spoke Quechuan, the Indian language.

"They say that two days ago their village was attacked," the interpreter said. "Some people came in and attempted to kill every man, woman, and child. These survivors managed to run and hide in the jungle until the battle was over. Then they walked all the way here—about twenty-five miles."

The La Drones, thieves and smugglers, infested the area; so we assumed it was the work of the La Drones.

The next morning we launched helicopters and flew to the village. Almost every man, woman, and child had been butchered. The most sickening sight was a pile of children's arms lying to one side. The buildings had been dynamited and burned. There was nothing left. It looked like a scene from the movie *Apocalypse Now.*

A few more survivors appeared out of the jungle. A young Peruvian man told us that a *Sendero* army had surrounded the town.

"Did they ask for money? Did they want something?" the Sergeant Major asked.

After the interpreter repeated the question, several in the group shook their heads.

A woman spoke up and talked for quite a long time.

Finally the interpreter related her story. "She says they didn't let anybody leave. They just started shooting. The people in the village tried to fight, but they killed everybody."

Eventually the whole story came out. It seems that a missionary had come to the village to give the children inoculations, so the communists had come in and cut off the arms of all those children who were inoculated. It was an old communist method of intimidation. They'd committed the same atrocities in Southeast Asia.

Only in this village they had gone one step farther. They had insisted that the children's parents do the amputating. If the parents didn't obey, they butchered the whole family. From the carnage I saw around me, it looked like that's exactly what had happened.

A change passed over the faces of the Special Forces men standing there.

They became very quiet, their faces hard, pained. Tears ran down the cheeks of a couple of the men. But they were tears of anger. If they ran into the *Sendero* again, there would probably be no survivors on their part.

It was no surprise to us that the enemy had left behind weapons and ammunition made by the Russians and Chinese. Although the Chinese disavowed any connections with the *Sendero*, we found their weapons after every encounter.

The surprise was finding weapons of the North Koreans. So we had a new player in the game. This was definitely not the work of the La Drones but the work of armed *Sendero* troops.

Within a few days the little girl with the big eyes was medivaced to Lima. A medic in Lima, Donnie, who was our doctor from time to time, got her on a flight to St. Jude's Hospital in the US.

A sergeant major and a Viet Nam multi-award winner, Donnie was the one who took charge and helped us rescue the DEA and Peruvian Police who were captured when we stumbled across the Colombian Lab. It was rumored that he'd been nominated twice for the Congressional Medal of Honor as a medic, and he'd managed to send several Peruvian children to St. Jude's. Children who had been burned, shot, or badly disfigured—cases the Peruvian doctors had given up on. He'd get a C130 diverted, and it would divert all the way back to St. Jude's by way of Panama. Within a few months these children would come back healthy and alive.

For a while things went smoothly at Maza Mari. I gained weight on the abundance of good food and made some new friends. One of those friends was a missionary pilot by the name of Chris Unger. He flew into our camp in a Maule airplane. That's a tail wheel aircraft made in the US and used by various non-government agencies, like the Iran-Contras. Originally from Georgia, Chris was a tall, gangly man in his late fifties. His job was to support the various missions in that part of the world.

A very pious man, he refused to carry weapons of any kind and always prayed over his meals, even if those meals were sea rations. I found an old case of Lurks, that's dehydrated military food, left over from forever. You have to put water in it and lay it in the sun to warm it up.

Chris acted like that was the greatest gift in the world, so much better than the food he had been eating. He even prayed over that.

Since I had worked on Maule aircraft in the past, I sometimes made minor repairs on Chris's plane, so we became friends.

Then one day Chris landed and came running up to my shop, wide-eyed and breathless.

"Some people need help," he said, "out at La Mission. Somebody's got to get over there right away."

We went together to the office.

"I was supposed to take some supplies to La Mission today," he told the sergeant major and some others who had followed us in, "but—."

"La Mission?" the commander interrupted. "They've got a hospital there, don't they?"

"Yes, a hospital and a school. It's a Catholic mission, run by the Belgians. They've got a hospital and a school. There's a priest there and some nuns and school teachers."

He stopped and took a deep breath and, trembling, wiped his palms on his pants.

"When I landed at La Mission, I noticed that there were some men there with guns. I was going to taxi up and shut the engine down, but they raised their guns and started shooting at me. So I whipped the plane around and took off."

"Were these men Indians?"

He kind of laughed at that. "No, the Indians in the area don't even have guns—just stone knives and bows and arrows. They still wear robes and have tattoos all over their bodies. These men were not Indians. Probably the *Sendero*."

The base commander decided to launch a mission, but first we had to get satellite photographs and figure the distances to fly with the helicopters. La Mission was a good distance from our base, so we couldn't do it in one trip. We had to do it in stages. As quickly as we could, we filled helicopters with 55 gallon drums of fuel, flew out and set up a couple of fuel dumps. However, it took two days to get the fuel dumps in place.

Finally we took off in three helicopters, each containing 2 ex-pat crew members, 2 Peruvian gunners and 6 SF and Sinchis as passengers. I went as a first officer in one of the helicopters, and we arrived at La Mission at about 10:30 in the morning.

When we circled the village, making a combat approach, we saw people on the ground moving quickly into the jungle, except for a man who stood on the soccer field waving his arms like mad.

The first helicopter touched down, and the Sinchis and SF peeled out and secured the area. Roberts, the SF officer I'd met my first day at Maza Mari, and I were on the second helicopter. Then the third helicopter came in.

When we shut the helicopters down, we heard people leaving in motorboats on the river. The man who had been waving his arms ran up to the Sinchis and SF and to each one of the helicopters with tears in his eyes. "Thank you! Thank you! You saved my life! The communists were going to kill me."

At one time the village must have been very pretty. It even had a fountain and a clock tower. But the church and hospital had been blown up and burned.

"One of the teachers is still in that building over there," the man told the SF. He pointed at a small building—one of the few still standing. "They've been killing a teacher every day. There are only two of us left."

Roberts and a couple of the other SF went to the building, but the door was locked.

"We're Americans," Roberts yelled. "We're going to get you out of there. We're going to break down the door, so stand back."

When they got in, they brought out a slender lady in her 20's or 30's. She was crying and gasping for breath. Roberts put his arm across her shoulders, partly to comfort her, partly to hold her up.

"You're safe now," he kept saying, and the other teacher came over to translate because she didn't know English.

She had long blond hair and under normal circumstances was probably an attractive woman. But her dress was crumpled like she'd been sleeping in it, and there were dark circles under her eyes.

Every time she tried to talk, she started crying again.

By now some of the Indians had come out of the jungle, small men and women, clothed in brown robes that looked kind of like dresses. They had tattoos on their faces, arms, and hands and carried bows and arrows, spears, and blowguns. They'd been fighting to rescue the teachers as best they could against the automatic weapons of the *Sendero* and had even managed to kill some of the enemy. The *Sendero* were very brave when they were fighting against people who couldn't defend themselves; but the minute the Sinchis and SF arrived, they ran.

A couple of the native women went to the teacher and put their arms around her.

"There were ten teachers here," the male teacher told us. "Every day at noon they took one of us to the soccer field and made a big speech. Then they'd either shoot the teacher or cut his head off."

"Where are the nuns and the priest?" Roberts asked.

"They killed the priest," he said. "I think the nuns are dead too." But he asked the Indians, then told Roberts that the priest and the nuns had been taken into the jungle.

The captain's eyes turned to ice. He sent squads down the major trails to look for them.

I waited on board the helicopter with the rest of the crew; and while we waited, the Indians brought some coconut milk and dried fish to the open doors of the helicopters. They held these gifts out one at a time, cupping them in both hands, meaning that these were very special gifts—their way of saying "thanks." And I accepted the food with both hands to acknowledge my reverence of the gift. Then after we had eaten, we gave the Indians some of our food.

The squads returned within a couple of hours and said they'd found no sign of the nuns or the priest. They had probably been taken into the jungle and raped and tortured. The *Sendero* took great delight in torturing people before they killed them.

"Where did these people come from?" the captain asked the Indians.

They pointed at the river and told the interpreter they'd come from a village five or six miles downstream.

The SF and Sinchis got in the three helicopters, and we lifted off and went to the village and landed on gravel bars at the river. I sat in the helicopter with the other crew members while the Peruvians and SF went to the village. From what we could see there were no men there.

Before long we heard shots coming from the *Sendero* who were hiding in the jungle, shots and screams. The Sinchis and SF searched the huts; and if they found Sendero literature or weapons, they burned those huts and the ammunition inside flared and exploded. Then the SF came back to the river and destroyed the *Sendero's* canoes by shooting the outboard motors and knocking holes in the boats. It wouldn't take the communists long to build more canoes, but in the meantime, it would help to immobilize them.

Finally, we went back to La Mission to pick up the two school teachers.

Weeping, the teachers hugged the Indians and said their goodbyes and got on board with the few possessions they could find amidst the rubble.

These were people, the priest, the nuns and teachers, who had given up 3 or 4 years or more of their lives to go to the jungle to help the Indians there. A lot of good people had died. We wished we could have done more.

A FEW MONTHS later, just before I left Maza Mari, Chris flew in and said nothing was left of the village. All the people who had stayed there were dead. The *Sendero* had come back and totally destroyed the village and finished massacring anybody they could find.

They were a very bloodthirsty lot—especially if the odds were 10 to 1 in their favor—very brave when there were a large number of them and one of you and you had no gun. Cowards if you were armed.

A year later some of us flew near La Mission and diverted so we could fly over the area. The jungle was reclaiming the ruins. Except for part of the fountain and clock tower, there was no evidence that anything had ever been there. No evidence of all the good work that had been done.

WHEN I FINALLY returned to Santa Lucia, the other ex-pats and I became better and better at confiscating planes. The bounty on my head and the heads of the other pilots hit a quarter of a million dollars. We'd gone from $50,000 to $150,000 to $250,000. The bounty on the helicopters was $500,000--a fortune to the local people.

Needless to say, it was very dangerous for a helicopter to go down in *Sendero* territory, but that's exactly what happened to the helicopter I was on only a month after I returned to Santa Lucia.

Part Seven:
Down in Enemy Territory

Chapter Twenty-Two

ONCE WE WERE hauling supplies over the mountains by helicopter from Lima, flying at 14,000 feet. On board were barrels of fuel, personal items, food, and, of course, the crews of the helicopters.

Since old Bell helicopters weren't built to go to 14,000 feet, I had disconnected the pressure relief valve so it would develop power above its normal operating altitude. Then I took a coke can and made a blocking plate out of it—a trick used in the high mountain country like Alaska and Colorado. I didn't have to worry about taking the can out later because the pressure after about 20 hours eats the aluminum and blows the can out the exhaust stack.

Four helicopters made up the mission that day. We always traveled in groups of two, three, and four when we went on any long cross-country missions so we could provide help for each other.

As we neared the crest of the mountain, a radio call came from the first helicopter, "Mayday. Mayday. Mayday. We're in trouble."

Those of us in the second helicopter watched as the first helicopter started going down, the rotor blade almost stopped. It was just carrying too big of a load to make it over and impacted just below the top of the mountain. Fortunately, it didn't burn on impact, but a fire could start at any time.

"We've got to help them. We're going to land," Flash said. He was our pilot that day. "Get off and take all the equipment off. I'm going to take the helicopter on up the mountain."

It wasn't easy, but we landed on the side of the mountain and immediately started tossing all the equipment off, while the other two helicopters provided circling protection, in case the enemy came after us.

Then Flash took the helicopter on up to the top of the mountain and landed on a plateau just above where the other helicopter had crashed.

He told us later, that what he found when he climbed down to the crash site broke his heart. The crew on the mountain was in bad shape. They had all been injured. But Underdog was on that particular helicopter. Even though his leg was broken, though he'd injured his back and arm, he was a guardian. He had to do something.

The fuel tank had broken open and covered the whole crew, so the most immediate danger was fire. Underdog must have started hauling everybody off the helicopter immediately, starting with the flight engineer, who had broken arms and legs and whose right eye was lying on his cheek and whose head was partially caved in.

Underdog had unbuckled the guy, pulled him out of the seat, and dragged him down the side of the mountain, away from the helicopter. He placed the eye back in the socket and stopped the bleeding as best he could.

Then, crawling or scooting somehow on his right leg, he went back for the captain and dragged him down the mountain too. Because the captain was having trouble breathing, Underdog put an esophageal airway down his throat before going back to the helicopter for the first officer.

He had broken ribs, a broken pelvis, a broken leg, and severe damage to one knee. After making the first officer as comfortable as he could, he went back for the two gunners. Both had broken legs and ribs.

By the time Flash arrived on the scene, Underdog was trying to perform first aid on each of the crew members—attending the ones most likely to live first. The most critical injuries that could be treated, he had treated.

"What can I do?" Flash asked.

"I've about got it."

Flash watched as Underdog shot some of his patients full of morphine to relieve their pain. "Are you going to give yourself an injection? Looks like you're hurt pretty bad too."

Underdog shook his head and put his medical supplies away.

"Let me help you up the mountain."

"Oh, no. Take the flight crew first."

So Flash put the flight engineer over his shoulder in a fireman's carry, took him up the mountain and put him in our helicopter. Then he came back down for the next person and the next, until he got everybody but Underdog on board.

Like a fool Underdog tried to walk.

"What are you doing? You can't walk. You're just hurting yourself."

Flash grabbed Underdog and carried him too. Then he had six people aboard a helicopter that was sitting on top a mountain.

Flash radioed us. "I'm going to fly these people back to Lima. I'll send another helicopter in for you guys. Protect the crash site."

He fired up the engine and with maximum power plus got it into a hover. Then he dived down the side of the mountain to get up air speed, and away he went.

The only fatality from that crash was the flight engineer. All the other men survived—mainly because of the heroic actions of Underdog and Flash Gordon.

Underdog stopped by Santa Lucia several months later and came limping into my shop, his hair gray like the rest of us. Maybe I'd just hadn't noticed that he was getting gray, but it seemed like his hair had turned gray overnight. We hugged like brothers.

He walked with a cane, so he was forced to retire and go back to the states. When Underdog got on the plane that afternoon, one of the crew he'd pulled off the helicopter wept because Underdog had saved his life.

Luckily the *Sendero* did not come after us while we sat on the side of the mountain waiting for another helicopter to arrive. In fact, we didn't see another person on that mountain, but we weren't quite so lucky when the *Sendero* shot our helicopter down a few weeks later.

Chapter Twenty-Three

BECAUSE OF THE high bounty placed on the helicopter and those on board, we picked up fire every time we flew out. Fortunately, it's very hard to shoot a helicopter down. It isn't hard to disable one once it is on the ground, but it isn't easy at all to shoot one out of the air. However, helicopters often came home riddled with bullet holes. One of my last jobs in the evening was to patch those holes.

A few weeks later we had to fly two helicopters on a mission deep in the jungle using our global navigation system. The helicopter I was on consisted of Polecat as captain, Scott and Raol as gunners, and I was the crew chief. Our first officer was Erick, a tall, blond, blue-eyed Peruvian of Swiss ancestry and a major in the Peruvian military.

While we were flying over a *Sendero* village, bullets hit the helicopter. Then the engine light came on.

"We've lost power," Polecat yelled into his headset to the other helicopter. "We're going down."

I braced myself as the helicopter went into auto rotation.

"Roger," a voice came over the radio, "we'll provide protection."

As soon as we sat down in tall grass, I disconnected my headset and jumped out. Polecat followed me to the back of the helicopter, where we opened the cowling doors. Oil covered everything. The engine had probably toasted out.

"The engine's gone," I told Polecat.

"We've got company coming!" Erick shouted. "About a hundred of them and they're armed!"

The other helicopter circled overhead, firing machine guns to keep the people who were coming at bay.

"We'll have to destroy everything!" Polecat yelled.

Raol and Scott handed me cans of machine gun ammunition, and I put them on the ground. Eric started shooting our high tech radios and all the other equipment with his pistol.

"You can't land," Polecat yelled into a hand-held radio. "You'd be a sitting duck. We'll have to run. What's the pick up point?"

I opened the fuel tank and took three thermite grenades off my pistol belt.

"Roger. Zebra. What's the best way to get there?" Polecat asked. "What's the—? Okay." He stuck the radio in his vest and pointed west.

The others took off, Raol and Scott carrying the machine guns on their shoulders, Eric and Polecat carrying cans of ammunition.

"Is everybody clear?" I yelled.

I pulled the pins on two grenades and threw them inside the helicopter and pulled the pin on the third grenade and dropped it in the gas tank. Then I ran. Seconds later explosions rocked the earth, and I felt the heat of the fire against my back.

I chased after the others, fighting my way through grass that was tall, like Buffalo grass—sometimes up to my waist—sometimes over my head. But there was razor grass in that particular valley as well. Razor grass can cut and scratch you and make infected wounds on your arms, hands, and feet. It can actually cut through your clothing.

The other helicopter was still shooting rounds of ammunition at the ground in front of our pursuers, but it wouldn't be able to stay with our crew much longer, or it would just be a beacon telling the enemy where we were.

I soon caught up to the others because they were carrying the machine guns and ammunition. It wasn't long before they were winded and had to stop.

Polecat wiped sweat out of his eyes. "We're going to have to leave the guns. They're too heavy."

"How far we got to go?" Raol asked.

"It's about 30 kilometers. Point Zebra. Top of a hill. We just head for the setting sun."

"Well, let's take these things apart," Scott said. "We can't leave these guns like this."

So Scott and I pulled the barrels out of the guns and used them to beat on the housing, bending the barrels in the process so the guns would no longer function. The others opened the ammunition cans. Then we made a pile of the guns and ammo.

Polecat, Erick, Raol, and Scott ran off again as I got my last thermite grenade and tossed it on the pile. Then I ran.

Soon the grenade went off followed by the explosions of bullets going off in all directions. It sounded like someone had set off a string of huge firecrackers.

We all knew what we were supposed to do in case a helicopter went down—get to a pickup point, which in this case was Zebra, a flat, clear area on a hill, an area that didn't have a lot of trees where people could hide and snipe at us. We knew if we could survive long enough, the guardians would come and get us. But we had to get to the extraction point first.

I traveled light, with just my weapons—a rifle hung over my shoulder, two pistols—and lots of ammunition. I'd used all my grenades but two fragmentary grenades and two smoke grenades. I had some food, a little water, and some water purifying tablets packed inside my vest. We didn't have an Emergency Locator Transmitter with us, because the enemy would hear it and fix our position. We had four days maximum to get to the pickup point, or we'd be written off as dead.

When we'd put about 3 kilometers between ourselves and the crash site, the other helicopter left. That meant our pursuers were about three kilometers behind us, and they would be coming fast. These people wanted us bad—wanted our heads—wanted that money.

They knew the general direction we'd taken—toward the setting sun. The sun was our basic guideline, and the pickup point was quite a few kilometers away.

The two Peruvian officers, Raol and Erick, were just as motivated as we were to get away. They had the same price on their heads that the Americans had. Because they were with DEA agents, they were counted as gringos.

When we got out of the tall grass, we found ourselves by a swamp, because the area was a flood plane during the rainy season.

"We're leaving prints," Scott said, when we slowed down, to catch our breath.

I had to wipe the sweat out of my eyes before I could see anything. It was a hot day and the humidity must have been 100%.

"We don't have time to leave evasive trails. Or disguise our prints." Polecat hurriedly scanned the area. He pointed to the right. "Let's go that way—toward the swamp."

We veered off to the right and ran along the edge of the swamp, which was thick with trees. Before long we found ourselves in soft, oozy mud. Now we were definitely leaving footprints.

So we entered the swamp and waded deep into it, loosing ourselves in the thick trees and in the brush that grew in the more shallow areas.

Erick and I froze as a snake swam past and headed off into a thicket of saplings.

Peru only has three varieties of snakes that are not poisonous. The rest are. The problem with those that are not poisonous is that they, like the anaconda, are big. They are large and vicious and eat small animals and will attempt to attack a human being.

Peru also has piranhas.

The books say that there is no record of piranhas attacking a live human being; but if you ask the natives, they will all tell you stories of piranhas attacking and killing somebody they knew and stripping the body of all flesh.

Just a few weeks before a Peruvian Air Force Twin Otter had to land not too far from the area we were in, except that the Twin Otter had landed in a lake. An air force officer whose wife died aboard that aircraft said the crew and passengers had been attacked by piranhas and only six of the twenty people on board had survived until rescue. They had either been killed in the plane crash or attacked by the piranhas, their bodies literally ripped apart by hundreds of thousands of little fish with vicious teeth.

The water we were in was backwater—very murky and muddy. Most of the streams in Peru were clear, almost pristine. But because the water was murky, it probably contained every known disease, every known bacteria in the world—plus snakes, plus piranhas, plus leeches.

As soon as we got far into the swamp area, we immediately walked back up stream in the direction we'd just come from. We walked a good kilometer. Then we found some logs and parts of tree roots that were out of the water a little so we'd have some cover and some protection from the snakes and piranhas and leeches and whatever else might be there.

We formed a crude circle, 10 to 20 feet apart, so we could put up crisscross firing positions. If people came from any direction, we'd see them approaching.

But the tall grass along the edge of the swamp and the bushes and trees growing in the water made it almost impossible for anyone outside the swamp to see us.

I found a dead tree with branches sticking out of the water that I thought would offer some concealment and took out camouflage makeup and smeared it on my face before I hunkered down in the tepid water and mud. We tried to make ourselves very small and tried not to even breathe as we waited for the people behind us to catch up.

Within a few minutes we heard them crashing through the brush, following the footprints we'd left earlier along the outskirts of the swamp. Mosquitoes buzzed around my head and bit me through the makeup.

I'd thrown my helmet aside as I ran away from the helicopter and was wearing my camouflage hat with a head net stored inside it. But I hadn't had time to take it out and put it on. Next time, I decided, I'd use mud instead of the makeup. Mud offered better protection from insects.

Our pursuers were talking and tromping around. A couple of people fired bullets off into the swamp, hoping we'd return fire or they'd hit somebody close and that person would scream. This was a technique the Russians had taught them.

The *Sendero* often drove down the roads and fired their weapons into the brush and trees. If anybody fired back, they would attack.

Some of the pursuers came back upstream; some went downstream, looking for footprints coming out of the swamp. They were too afraid to go into it. They knew there were poisonous snakes. They knew there were piranhas. They also knew they would get very sick if they went into the swamp. However, we had no choice. Though Rambo makes it look easy to stand and fight 60 or 70 people, it would have actually been impossible.

After about three hours we didn't hear any more noise. But instead of jumping up and starting to move, we stayed in place another two hours to make sure there wasn't somebody sitting out there in the grass waiting for us to make some noise or reappear.

While we waited, very carefully, very quietly, we occasionally took a drink or ate a little food. We didn't have much food or water with us. We had water purification tablets, but they had to sit in the water for three hours to be effective.

I smeared some mud on my face. Then I quietly covered my head with netting.

Just as it was beginning to get dark, we got up very carefully and started forward, moving in the direction of our pickup point, using the shuffle step, going slowly and quietly, sliding one leg in front of the other in the water so we wouldn't make any splashes.

We decided to keep going forward in the swamp through twilight, so we walked another 7 or 8 kilometers, wadding in water up to our knees in some places and up to our chests in other places.

It was summer. The temperature was typically about 90 degrees and the humidity close to 100%, so I was sweating. I was dripping. Dripping wet all the time.

I'd lost so much water though and had so little to drink, that I felt no need to urinate. I was thankful about that. We didn't dare pee in the swamp water because microscopic bacteria in the water would climb the stream of urine, enter our kidneys, and infect them.

But it was much better to be wading in infested water, dripping wet than to be dead or tortured. The people in that area had a history of torturing people before they cut their heads off.

The helicopter, even though it was burned out, would pay them half a million dollars. The Narco Traffickers always paid off on a downed helicopter. Money didn't mean anything to them.

Those pursuing us knew that anybody they could catch was worth at least $50,000. Since there were five members of the crew, they'd be paid at least 750,000 US dollars for the helicopter and the heads of the crew. Not only was the $750,000 a fortune to those people, they'd also have all the glory and rewards the drug lords could heap on them.

Some of the crew though, like Polecat and me, would be worth a lot more than that.

When it got so dark we couldn't see, we made a second camp. Not up on the land though. We found a second spot much like the first spot, where we set up firing stations and spent the night in the swamp.

Chapter Twenty-Four

I SAT DOWN in the water, behind a log. All through the night small fish nibbled on my clothing. I couldn't slap them away because they might be piranhas and might decide to attack, but I knew that if I had any cuts on my body, if the razor grass had cut through my fatigues and slashed my skin, the piranhas would attack anyway—hundreds of them.

The water was warm, and the air heavy—heavy with moisture and the smell of rotting compost and rotting animals.

Soon it was dark, so dark we could hardly see anything.

We took turns staying awake for about an hour and a half apiece, so somebody was always awake. We had to wake up anyone who was snoring. Since I have a tendency to snore, I didn't get much sleep that night.

When daybreak came, we waited until we could see clearly. Tall grass still stood along the edge of the swamp, and the area was still thick with trees. So we were fairly well concealed.

Polecat consulted his map and compass, and we moved out slowly and walked probably another 3 or 4 kilometers, using the shuffle step again. It was slow and arduous going.

Muddy water came up to our waists in places, and our feet slid forward through soft mud. When we walked, the water became even muddier. But I figured the mud was our friend because, after it had settled, it would not give even a good tracker an indication of where we had passed.

Finally, we sent Erick, our first officer, up on shore. He didn't see anyone around, so at about 10:00 in the morning, we decided we could make better time if we got up on dry land.

When we climbed out of the swamp, we were a grim looking crew, wet and muddy with camouflage makeup and mud smeared on our faces, holding weapons at the ready. We almost scared each other.

The terrain was changing, becoming more rugged, more hilly and rocky. In fact, we spotted a rocky area on the side of a hill a half-mile or so ahead that would be a good area to get to. We could walk on the rocks and if we didn't move the rocks around, wouldn't leave much of a trail. But we still had to be very alert.

Our enemies would not give up easily. If they found the gringos, they could be wealthy—have nice homes, televisions, and mopeds. They might even be able to move to New York City, where a large number of Peruvians had already moved. So they were highly motivated.

On land we moved quietly because we didn't want to disturb the birds. When birds in wilderness areas hear anything, they become very quiet. Then if they hear anything else, they take flight. So if you are looking for a group of men and the forest goes silent, it's a good indication that those men are around; and if you see birds take to the air, you can bet the men you are looking for are in that area.

Scott and I didn't have the Daniel Boone skills that the guardians had, but we were the only ones with hunting experience, so we went ahead to scout the area. I circled off to the left and Scott circled off to the right.

I listened for the birds, for the sounds of people talking. The Peruvians liked to chatter when they were hunting someone. It seemed to give them courage.

I crept forward to the cover of trees or bushes and then stopped, scanning the area for footprints, bent grass, and movement. Peruvians also like their cigarettes, so I was alert for the smell of cigarette smoke, which carries quite a distance. All the time I was being careful not to leave tracks myself.

Finally, I slipped up to the rocky area then climbed on up the hill and found a spot where I could search the countryside with my binoculars—looking for birds taking flight—looking for movement. Far off in the distance I made out a woman carrying a basket or something on her head. Closer to the swamp I saw a couple of men carrying guns, but they were going in the opposite direction.

Soon Scot joined me.

"Did you see anything?"

He shook his head. "Not a thing."

"Go ahead and signal the others."

He flashed a mirror at them.

After they'd joined us, we all walked for a while on the rocky terrain, which wasn't too far away from the swamp. If we had to, we could go back to it.

We traveled as quietly as possible, so quietly that the birds in the trees didn't miss a beat. That meant we traveled very slowly as well. *Sendero* camps dotted the area which meant mines dotted the area as well; thus we also had to be alert for booby traps and mines. Every now and then I went ahead of the group to make sure no one was ahead of us, and Scott dropped behind, so we could warn the others if people were gathering close to us.

At the middle of the day we took a short break. We were hot, hungry, thirsty, and tired and were very low on water and food. Early that morning I'd drunk the last of my water and later my only coke. Before leaving the swamp, I'd filled my collapsible water bottle and added the purifying tablets. The water still didn't look very good and had debris in it but was probably safe to drink by then.

It didn't taste much better than it looked, but I made a meal of an energy bar and bad tasting water. Then we started out again.

Toward the end of that day, we gathered in the shade of some trees.

Scott looked worried when he caught up to us. "I think someone's on our trail. I climbed a ridge and caught sight of birds circling the area a few miles back and thought I saw movement in the trees."

"Do you guys think we should head back to the swamp now?" Polecat asked.

I'd been scouting ahead and shook my head. "As soon we get over this hill and start down the other side, the swamp will be closer to us. But it will still be several hundred feet away. Why don't you guys go on? I'll put out a booby trap."

They moved off and were soon lost in the trees.

I'd saved my coke can, so I cut it in half. It was the perfect size to fit a grenade into. I had two smoke grenades. They have instantaneous detonators; whereas, the fragmentary grenades have delayed detonators. So I carefully exchanged a detonator from one of the smoke grenades for the detonator on a fragmentary grenade and carefully removed the pin. Then holding the spoon back, I slipped the fragmentary grenade inside the can.

Finally, I packed the can in dirt, tied a plastic fishing line to the spoon as a trip wire, and laid the line across the trail. When the grenade came out of the can, it would go off.

About an hour later, we heard the explosion, followed by a large number of automatic weapons firing in every direction. We had an army of people following us, and those people weren't that far back because we were only traveling one or two miles an hour. And we still had about 15 kilometers to go to reach the pickup point.

We decided to go back to the swamp, because that was the area these people were afraid of. So that night we were back in the swamp, back in the water and mud and whatever else might be there. Back to the rotting grass and rotting leaves. Back to the sour stink of decaying vegetation and animals.

Chapter Twenty-Five

WE COULDN'T HELP but leave some footprints around the edge of the swamp where we went in. So Scott and Raol put anti-personnel bombs in the water around the perimeter of our second watery camp—about 50 yards upstream and downstream—the same type of bombs we had used in Nicaragua. They look kind of like golf balls; and if you step on one, it will blow a foot off. They put up sticks to mark where the bombs were so we wouldn't step on them when we left.

The second night was more miserable than the first. Maybe it was just that I was sick of the swamp, of the mud, of the smell, of the bugs.

I was sure I heard a hundred snakes sliding through the water and was attacked by thousands of bugs. Some of those insects—like the mosquitoes—tried to bite right through my clothing. The head net kept them out of my ears, nose, and eyes and kept them from biting my face. But there wasn't anything I could do about my hands. I'd lost my gloves sometime that first day. Probably when I took them off to grenade the helicopter. But I had to keep my gun and ammunition out of the water. Had to be ready to fire if the enemy discovered us.

I couldn't make any noise. Couldn't swat at those monsters. Besides, it wouldn't have done any good. There were too many.

That night we all slept fitfully.

The next morning as soon as we could see to move out, we did, heading through the swamp in the direction of the pickup point which was still 15 kilometers away. I'm not sure how far we'd gone when we heard one of the anti-personnel bombs go off. Then we heard screams. We stopped and looked back in the direction of the bombs.

"They're awful close," Raol said, his eyes wide.

Once again we also heard automatic weapons going off, as well as shotguns and rifles, being fired in every direction. Fortunately not in our direction. The hounds were still trying to chase us down.

"I think we'd better get up on dry ground," Polecat whispered as we gathered around him. Make a run for it, or they're going to catch us."

"Let's do it," Raol said excitedly. "They want that moneys."

"Besides, time is running out," Erick said. "They're going to write us off if we don't make it to Zebra soon. How long have we been out here? Three days or four?"

Scott shrugged. "Who knows? Seems like a week."

Polecat grinned and looked like a grinning ape with the all the mud smeared on his face. "Tomorrow will be four. So let's go."

We walked forward in the swamp until we found a log to step out on. A good tracker would probably find our prints, but it was the best we could do.

We started off at a run but stayed close to the swamp. We ran 50 yards or so and then walked 50 yards or so then ran again. After about an hour though, we fell on the ground and gasped for air. We were completely depleted. We were tired. We needed sleep. We'd eaten very little and drunk very little water.

The containers we used for collecting swamp water were fairly small, and we always had to wait 3 hours to take a drink. We were loosing a lot of water because we were perspiring constantly, especially when we started running.

The swamp water had rotted holes in our clothing, and one of my boots was coming apart at the toe.

We took turns scouting the area ahead and checking the back trail, so there was always someone ahead and someone behind.

At a certain time every day an observation plane—a quiet plane—flew over. It was called a quiet plane because it was designed with special propellers and a special exhaust system so that it made almost no noise. It could fly at 30,000 feet or 300 feet and contained very strong cameras. It would be used to track our progress.

Because we didn't have any emergency Locator Transmitters with us, it was our responsibility to get to the extraction point. We had been moving very, very slowly, so when we decided to run, we ran for all we were worth.

All of a sudden Raol, who was in the back caught up with us and frantically motioned at us to stop. We froze in place for a moment, listening and soon heard voices, people coming up behind us and to our right.

We couldn't see anyone because the trees and brush hid these people from view, but we slipped farther into the brush and froze in place while they passed. Then we stayed there for a couple of hours to make sure the people we'd heard had left the area before heading back to the shallows of the swamp and walking slowly forward again.

Finally, we came to open ground. No trees. No cover. We'd been following a compass. We'd been following our map. We had a pretty good idea that we were about 5 kilometers from the extraction point. When we crossed the open area, we had to be especially vigilant because we might have to fight. With that many people after us, we'd be dead in a few minutes.

As we moved out, we saw the quiet bird come overhead, so we ran and walked, ran and walked until we made it up the hill to the extraction point. Erick laid a piece of florescent cloth—international orange—on the ground, in the form of an "L," meaning, "Landing Zone."

Then we concealed ourselves as best we could behind some rocks and small trees and waited for the quiet bird to fly over again. About 45 minutes later, the pilot flew over and wagged his wings. Then he turned back and wagged his wings again. We'd been sighted.

We expected to see a helicopter coming after us, but we didn't see one or hear one. What we did see was a man who stood up from behind a rock.

We pointed our weapons at him, and my stomach tightened. If the enemy had found us, all the helicopters would pick up were our headless bodies.

But the man waved and walked forward. It was Antonio.

Then about half a dozen of our guardians come walking over the top of the hill. They'd been in hiding near the extraction point for the past three days, when they got word from the quiet bird that the helicopter crew had made it to Zebra point.

The guardians were there to protect us. They had automatic weapons in case we came under fire. They were professional soldiers—former Special Forces or former Navy Seals. Those guys were good. And we were awfully glad to see them.

The guardians waved. We waved back.

Antonio picked up a radio and made a call. Then the helicopters came in.

Of course, helicopters always make a racket, but the big old Hueys are especially loud. The main rotor blades pop and go, "Whoop, whoop, whoop, whoop," as they come in.

They attract people from miles around. The self-appointed army that had been chasing us was only a few miles behind. It would immediately come rushing to the area, so as the first helicopter came in and hovered, those of us who had been on the downed helicopter jumped on board very quickly. Then a second helicopter came in to pick up the guardians, and we all went back to our base.

PRETTY BOY LAUGHED when Scott and I came walking in the tent, probably at the way we looked. "Wow! You made it back!" he said, then put his fingers to his nose. "But get out of here. You guys stink."

Flash ran in and patted me on the back. "I knew Larazus would make it. But did you have to wait until the third day again? We'd about given up on you."

"Whew!" One of the other guys in the tent grinned and backed away from us, fanning his face. "I'll talk to you guys later. After you get a bath. You smell like garbage."

My clothes were rotting off my body. My boots had slit open from being in that muck for so long. When I took them off, my socks fell off in pieces.

I had lesions on my skin from the bacteria and scratches I'd picked up. I'd also picked up various types of fungus, especially on my toes and feet.

At Santa Lucia the water for showers was loaded into a tank and then warmed by the sun. At the end of the day everybody would come up to get a shower, and for the first couple of people the water would be kind of tepid or warm. When I got in the shower that afternoon, I scrubbed my entire body with a scrub brush; and the water got icy before I was finished. But I didn't care because I was washing off all that stink.

Part Eight:
The Battle of Santa Lucia

Chapter Twenty-Six

EVERY NOW AND then the *Sendero* or Narco Traffickers would decide they needed to attack the gringo camp and the national police in their area, and with rare exceptions their attacks followed the same pattern.

They would wait until there was a full moon and good weather. They didn't like attacking in the rain. Their attacks always came from the same direction and always on a Friday or Saturday night. They weren't very good soldiers, and they didn't have enough weapons.

What they did have was whistles and horns, which they blew to scare the gringos. As a result the gringos could hear them coming for forty-five minutes. The battle was like a big party to them, and they were usually drunk and high on cocaine.

Along the east side of the Santa Lucia base stretched a river, and in the river sat an island. The *Sendero* or Narco Traffickers, whoever was attacking that night, would sneak in and set up machine guns or rockets and fire into the camp from across the river and from the island.

When we'd first arrived, we were given an Emergency Evacuation Plan. The embassy gave us a bunch of Mae West life vests—little inflatable vests that flight crews wear. If we were attacked, we were to go out in the river, inflate our Mae Wests, and swim out to the island and defend ourselves from there. Only the island was usually already in use—by the enemy.

So the embassy sent some people down to study the situation. These people finally decided there was no practical way to defend the base because the enemy had the high ground—all the way around us, with the river at our backs. If we came under fire, we were to "defend the Santa Lucia base as if it were the Alamo." That was not too encouraging because the people at the Alamo lost, with no survivors except for a couple of women and children.

One night the *Sendero* fired a bunch of Rocket Propelled Grenades into our camp, grenades that had been supplied by the Chinese or Russians or Czechoslovakians. They were excellent weapons, but they didn't go off because they'd forgotten to pull out the firing pins. That particular night not one of them had pulled the firing pins. Their training was very poor.

Usually when an attack was about to take place, we'd get an intelligence report from Los Palmos, a large palm plantation in the area.

On the weekends when the moon was full, we just assumed we were going to be attacked. So we loaded the helicopters with machine guns and ammunition—ready to take off at a moment's notice.

Then we'd watch a movie or play poker using Peruvian money, which changed every year or so. At first one Peruvian dollar would be worth one American dollar, but within a few months the ratio would be a million Peruvian dollars to one American dollar. We kept that money and had stacks of it—a foot or a foot and a half high. These stacks probably represented ten to fifteen dollars.

We'd play poker until 11:30 or so, then quit and lie down to sleep but in full combat dress with our rifles, pistols, or shotguns right by our sides. So when we heard the first gunfire, we went to our defense posts.

Because the Peruvians always blew whistles, we could tell when they were thirty minutes away, fifteen minutes away, and at the outer perimeter. About ten minutes before the attack was to begin, we put on night vision gear and checked the claymore mines to make sure they were pointing in the right direction.

Explosives and small ball bearings filled these mines making them like giant shotguns. We set them off with electric clackers.

My first job was to help launch the helicopters; then I went to my post behind a wall of sand bags that stood in front of my tent and defended the area from there, if necessary. These sandbags were stacked three or four layers deep around the tents. They would slow down smaller ammunition but would not stop .50 caliber bullets. Inside were firing steps and gun ports, so we could fire from 360 degrees off each of the sides.

When we saw movement on the island or across the river, we knew the enemy was in place.

We would wait, and here they would come—blowing their whistles, banging their horns, and blowing ooga horns. When they got to about 300 meters, we fired off some flares on parachutes so the Peruvians would know they'd been spotted. The Peruvians would shoot their guns a few times run. That was the height of the battle.

Then we would go to bed. The enemy was not going to come back. They didn't want to come back. That was the war for the night.

There were usually no casualties on either side. On rare occasions, they weren't drunk. On rare occasions, they had a leader or two, who maybe forced them to go into battle.

We heard that the front two or three ranks had weapons but the next three or four behind them had no weapons. When the person in front was killed, the one behind was supposed to pick up the rifle and continue the attack. Using this method, they could put up a pretty strong fight.

Then DEA would launch their helicopters and make sweeping turns, laying down machine gun fire. But usually all we had to do was set off the flares and put a few shots over their heads with the machine guns, and that was the end of the conflict.

The next day we'd search the area and pick up whatever we could find. A lot of times the Peruvians threw down their rifles before they ran. But the *Sendero* always threw down some flags.

These flags looked similar to the Soviet flag except that they had stars on them, and they were a way of warning the DEA. The enemy had been there. They had done their job. They had put out their flags. Maybe they'd even shot a few rounds of ammunition. Then it was over until the next full moon. We viewed these battles as comic relief.

We could be defensive but were not allowed to be offensive. That was against our rules of engagement. We could fight the *Sendero* and Narco Traffickers only if we were shot at, like in the early days of Viet Nam, when troops did not have bullets in their weapons until they were fired upon. Then the US troops were told to lock and load but only after they'd received permission to fight back.

So it became a big game.

Once in a while a sniper would shoot some of the workers, killing them or hurting them. The corps of workers was local people. If they were wounded, even a small wound, they had a pension for life from the Peruvian government and the US government. If they were shot and lived, they could retire. So there were always plenty of workers at the base, and they were very hard working people.

Then things began to change.

Chapter Twenty-Seven

FIRST, WE STARTED finding newer weapons after some of these battles and newer ammunition—most of it made by the North Koreans, military weapons, rather than the old shotguns and rifles we'd found before.

Once we captured a truck and on board was a truckload of 50-caliber ammunition. That meant our entire defensive operation at Santa Lucia Base had to be reconsidered because .50 caliber bullets could go right through the sand bags around our tents like they were slabs of butter.

We had to dig more slip trenches. We had to put up more concrete revetments, reinforced with steel, to provide a safe area from which we could fight. We knew we were in the valley of death, because they had the high ground.

For several weeks our intelligence organizations told us that the Narco Traffickers were bringing in Surface to Air Missiles or SAM7's, made by the North Koreans or the Russians, the same kind that had been used in Vietnam by the Vietnamese. These missiles would obviously be used to take out our transport aircraft.

The State Department sent a group of people to put additional avionics and additional equipment in our aircraft. They put flares and chaff aboard as well as missile lock equipment and some magic black boxes called IFF—Identify Friend or Foe systems—the same kind of high tech electronics being used in Desert Storm.

After a few weeks all our aircraft was updated, and we were trained in how to use the new technology. Then we could pop off a flare, and a heat-seeking missile would track off toward the flare instead of toward the helicopter's engine. The chaff was for metal-seeking missiles.

One day we were coming down the valley to Tingo Maria in four helicopters, traveling in formation. We tried to vary our route but didn't have a lot of space to do that between the mountains.

All of a sudden one of the IFF boxes lit up, meaning some type of radio signal was being beamed at our helicopters, and no alternate code said they were friends. So they had to be foes.

Then a couple of days later on the return trip two of the helicopters picked up a signal on the IFF.

But we weren't being shot at. No missiles came up at us.

So we elected to fly a little higher, which was not a good idea, because the higher you are, the easier it is for the missile to strike you. But if you're flying low, the people on the ground can shoot you.

We thought maybe the equipment was malfunctioning, but the avionics team checked it and said it was not. They concluded we'd picked up a stray radio signal. So we continued to make our daily runs back and forth, carrying people to various bases around the area.

Then one day we were flying four of our helicopters to Tingo Maria. Polecat was our pilot that day. Erick was the first officer, and I was sitting behind them as the crew chief. Irish and Snake were on board, as well as two gunners.

We were flying low, maybe 50 or 60 feet above the tree tops, when all of a sudden we started seeing tracers coming up at us. Every 5th bullet in a machine gun is a tracer, a phosphorous bullet that puts out a bright white, red, or yellow light, so the gunner can see where his bullets are going. We saw a lot of tracers. Then bullets started hitting our plane—high caliber bullets.

"I've been hit!" Erick screamed. Blood gushed out of his leg and foot.

Polecat looked back at me. "Get up here in front."

Snake and I grabbed Erick, unbuckled him out of his seat, and pulled him over into the back, where Snake started putting a tourniquet and compression bandage on his leg.

I climbed over into the front seat.

About that time more bullets came through the bottom of the aircraft, and the captain was hit in the right hand—the hand that operates the cyclic control. A couple of fingers were detached, and blood was squirting up.

"Take over. Take over. Take over."

So I was trying to maintain the helicopter with the lights on the IFF going up.

"Climb. Climb. Climb," came over the headset.

So all the helicopters started going up because we were under tremendous gunfire.

One of our gunners went down. Irish immediately pulled the door gunner out of his position, unhooked him from his fraidy belt, and climbed into his seat. He racked the bolt back on the .30 caliber and started returning gun fire, with the other door gunner doing the same thing.

The helicopter's radios were going absolutely crazy at this time, with all the pilots screaming at once.

"We're under fire! We're under fire! We have wounded! Climb! Climb! Climb!"

Meanwhile, all kinds of bullets slammed into our aircraft. They thumped through the thin aluminum then zinged through the cab.

We already had three wounded people aboard the helicopter and were under severe fire, so we started climbing, maximum power. But our old helicopters could only go up maybe 400-500 feet a minute because of the load they were carrying.

When we got to 4,000 feet, the enemy could still reach us, no problem.

About that time the IFF warning system came on showing that we had a radar lock on our helicopter.

"We have radar lock! We have radar lock!" the pilots screamed. "Avoid! Avoid! Avoid!"

We made sharp turns, climbed, went up as hard and fast as we could go.

One of the guardians had wrapped Polecat's hand, so he took over again.

Now the whole cockpit area was completely covered with blood from the first officer and the captain. We had broken windscreen, and still bullets whizzed through the entire helicopter, and we continued to climb.

"Smoke trail! Smoke trail!" somebody from the second or third helicopter back yelled.

That meant a missile was coming straight up at the four helicopters.

Immediately we punched the button that blew the chaff out of the way. These missiles weren't going for metal. They were going for heat. So we started popping flares and taking abrupt maneuvers to stay out of their way.

The first couple of missiles came by and went right on up. They have a surface ceiling of 14,000 or 15,000 feet. So we couldn't climb above them, we had to try to avoid them. Everybody was looking out the open doors, trying to spot more smoke trails.

Missiles travel at the speed of sound, so a poor little helicopter flying at 100 miles an hour is not going to outrun one. All we could do was pop more flares and try to avoid them.

About that time we flew over the next area, and here came more SAM7's.

The IFF warning signals were saying, "Turn right. Turn left. Climb. Dive."

"We're been hit by a missile!" Pretty Boy screamed from the third helicopter back.

Chapter Twenty-Eight

THERE WAS DEAD silence across the radios. Then Pretty Boy came back on. "I've still got a helicopter up. They got our tail rotor. I have no tail rotor."

We'd been popping flares, and the flares go slightly behind the aircraft where the tail rotor is located.

"I have no tail rotor. Half the tail is missing. We have a big, gaping hole in the back."

Pretty Boy was not the smoothest helicopter pilot I'd ever ridden with, but if anyone could fly a crippled aircraft, he could. He never gave up, no matter how bad the situation was.

The tail rotor is used for slow speed landings. It maintains stability. Otherwise when you try to land, you go into a gyroscopic jet and spin around and around until you loose control and spin into the ground. But if you maintain air speed, you can go ahead and fly, if the sink elevators are still operating.

We flew just as hard as we could to the Tingo Maria base because we were more than half way away from Santa Lucia.

We radioed Lima. "We're under attack. We're under attack. We have SAM7's. We have 50 calibers hitting our aircraft."

As we came into Tingo Maria, our helicopters were still working, so we landed inside the police compound. Except for Pretty Boy. He was back there trying to keep control of his helicopter so he could land at the Tingo Maria airport, using a run-on landing. That meant he'd have to maintain as much forward speed as possible, then instead of going into a hover, run the aircraft on the ground on the main skids.

As soon as we landed inside the base, I jumped out. In less than five minutes, a couple of guardians and I were at the main runway, a gravel and grass strip, with our rifles, pistols, and a large number of Peruvian police. As chief maintenance person and chief inspector on site, it was my job to get out there and see if I could do anything for the helicopter.

Pretty Boy, being a really good pilot, came in, and made his run-on, sparks flying off the gravel.

He literally ground the bottom of the landing skids off the aircraft by the time he stopped. But he brought it in. He had two injuries on board. All the helicopters had some wounded that day, men who had either picked up shrapnel fire or had picked up major wounds from 50 caliber bullets coming through the cockpits. We had blood in every one of the helicopters, and two of our Peruvian door gunners had died.

My job then was to see if I could get the helicopters patched up. A couple of the rotor blades had to be replaced. Pretty Boy's helicopter would have to have a whole new tail, so it would be down for two maybe three months.

We'd called for medivacs to send the wounded to Lima. We'd also called for reserve personnel. But we had to spend the night in Tingo Maria.

So that night we put the remaining helicopters inside the maintenance base and went to a "safe house" that the guardians had set up—a nice apartment complex located at the end of an alley, an apartment with thick walls, steel gates, and armed guards, land mines and claymores surrounding it. It reminded me of Fort Apache, with the gun ports of steel shutters that could be opened up in case of attack and machine guns on the roof.

"You know we should be dead," Irish kept saying.

And he was right. It was a well-planned attack, scattered down the valley like it was.

It took a lot to disturb Scott's laid-back, Gary Cooper demeanor, but Scott was definitely disturbed. "What's going on? That couldn't have been the peasants shooting at us. They've never been duck hunting. They don't know how to lead the aircraft."

Scott was right too. Usually all we had to do when we flew low was go as fast as the helicopter would go, so they'd only have a few seconds to hear the helicopter, point their weapons up, and start shooting. Then if we weren't gone by the time they fired, their bullets tore through the air behind us.

The next day we evacuated the wounded and the Peruvian Air Force showed up with four Toucans—fighter planes designed for close-in support—to fly air cover for us on our way back to Santa Lucia. If we came under attack, they were going to drop napalm and bombs. They were going to machine gun the area. So we were getting ready to go into a major battle.

We got one of the other aircraft we already had at Tingo Maria, got it equipped for flight, and once again started off with four helicopters.

Then we proceeded cautiously down the Rio Yialga Valley.

"Tracers! Tracers! Tracers!" someone yelled over the radio.

Suddenly we had tracers all around us and immediately did a 360 to fly back out of the area. We shoved the nose of the helicopter down to get the maximum air speed out of it and went back in the direction we'd come from to exit the fire zone. Then the four Peruvian fighter planes came in and started blasting away—plowing a path for us with their machine guns.

It didn't take long. Apparently as soon as the people below heard the 50 calibers firing at them instead of the 30 calibers, they took off and ran. Those who still could run.

We heard later that the Peruvian Air Force had killed somewhere between 30 and 50 of the enemy, judging from the weeping and crying that was taking place in the villages afterwards.

Within a few weeks some of our people who had been hurt, including our Peruvian first officer, started coming back to the base. We got together and had a party. We drank a toast to the dead. We drank a toast to the people who would never return to the valley, and we hoped like mad nothing that intense would ever happen again.

But something even stranger happened.

The enemy stopped attacking at all. On the weekends nobody came—no one attacked.

Finally, the base commander called us in for a meeting.

"We have some problems," he said. "The *Sendero* and Narco Traffickers have joined forces. They aren't attacking as often, but when they do attack, they're attacking as a well-trained military force. They know how to advance and cover. They know how to lay down their lines of fire. They know how to surround the encampment so the people inside can't escape."

We didn't know what to say. This certainly didn't sound like the men we'd been fighting.

"Not only that, they've been taking movies of their attacks and showing them over television."

He put on a video for us to watch.

One showed the *Sendero* attacking a police station and the police unable to defend themselves. It showed the *Sendero* setting the buildings on fire and the last policemen trying to get over the walls to run and being shot down. There were no survivors. The *Sendero* advanced and covered, advanced and covered, as if they were real soldiers. Not only that, they were wearing uniforms and carrying new weapons that had come out of North Korea.

"As you can see, these forces have been well trained and supplied. The Narco Traffickers are footing the bill and paying a lot of money. The North Koreans are supplying the arms."

"Anything happening around here?" I asked. "What's the intel from Los Palmos?"

"They say there are all kinds of troop movements in this area too. The people at Los Palmos are worried. They're bringing in more mercenaries to defend them."

We left the Operations Tent that night with feelings of trepidation.

The attacks on Santa Lucia during the next few months, on the rare occasions there were attacks, were more vicious, more efficient, more militaristic, less like a party and more like a battle than they had been before.

About that time several new DEA were hired. One of them was a tall, skinny kid who arrived in fatigues, combat boots, and beret. He wore a large gold chain around his neck and filled the air with obscenities. Occasionally around camp I heard a "hell" or a "damn," but this kid loved to shoot off his mouth.

His biggest problem though was that he liked to shoot off his guns, shooting them off where he shouldn't shoot them, pointing them at people. When he went into Lima, he bragged to the citizens in the restaurants and bars that he was with the DEA. He was scary. We all told the Base Commander, "Get this guy out of here." And he did.

Another of the new agents was also young. We nicknamed him Rambo because he worked out with weights every day and was a big guy with a fantastic physique. He also strutted around camp, bragging about how tough he was.

"Where are they getting these people?" I asked Scott one day as Rambo went strolling by flexing his muscles.

Scott grinned. "Well, now, partner, don't you feel safer with Rambo around?"

A couple of weeks later Flash and I were sitting in Benchley's Bar in Lima having dinner. The crowd was small compared to what it usually was.

Mr. Benchley, an Englishman who was married to a beautiful Peruvian lady, served American and British style food. His bar was a "time-out" area. If we had conflicts with other patrons, those conflicts didn't exist at Benchley's. It was a neutral zone where we could eat, drink, and relax.

Political conversations, conversations about the war, were not welcome. We just went there to get a meal, hear American or British music, and play darts or a little snooker. At first Mr. Benchley had a pool table, but he changed it to a snooker table because snooker was more British.

The ex-pats and DEA had a memorial at the bar. If one of our people got killed, we added his name to the memorial. We also put his name on a memorial at the International Airport. Sometimes these places were the only places our dead were recognized—except maybe at the Air American Museum in Texas.

Music played over a tape recorder, and the patrons picked out the tapes. Jimmy Bruffets, a Vietnamese singer, was one of the most popular selections because so many of the customers were Vietnam vets.

But somebody that night was a Tom Jones fan, so I was sitting there eating pork chops, Mr. Benchley's specialty, and listening to Tom Jones sing about how he was never going to fall in love again when Flash nudged me and pointed at three men who had just walked in. They looked European.

"Ever seen them before?" he asked.

Though they didn't look directly at us, they seemed aware of our presence as they casually crossed the room and sat down at a table by the wall. One of them, a tall, gaunt man with gray hair spoke with a distinct British accent when he ordered. The others appeared to be younger and one of them was a fairly small man with dark hair and looked like he might be French or Italian.

"Did you notice the way they walk? Their muscular condition?" I asked.

"Yeah, they're soldiers, aren't they? But what are they doing in Peru? They're not part of our group, and they're not National Police either. Any other government organizations here that you know of?"

I shook my head.

The following week I was back at Santa Lucia and spent most of my time under the bellies of various helicopters. I worked until late Friday night and all day Saturday then took off Sunday to rest. That night I had just gone to bed at about 1:00 when I heard machine guns firing. The lights in the tent went off immediately to give us cover.

Fortunately I had on my jeans and socks, so I just slipped on my boots and flight jacket, grabbed my rifle and shotgun and stepped outside.

When I left the tent, all I could see was tracers coming from across the river, from behind the base, from north, south, east, west, and every quarter in between. It looked like the fourth of July.

Chapter Twenty-Nine

I WENT TO my position behind a wall of sandbags, and a few moments later some of the guardians came running by.

"Stay at your posts," Snake yelled, "until we clear the area."

The guardians headed to one of the administration buildings, and we heard gunfire inside the camp. Some of the enemy was in the camp. Door to door and building to building fighting was going on all around us.

Soon Snake came back by and told us to go ahead and launch the helicopters.

Those of us who were mechanics or gunners formed human shields around the pilots and hurried to the helicopters and got them started. As soon as the helicopters were up, I ran back to my position at the sandbags in front of the tent; and the helicopters made clearing turns around the area, laying down gunfire all around the perimeters of the camp and outside the camp. That drove those outside the camp away. But the ones inside the camp were determined to fight.

So the mechanics had to make a second run to the helicopters when they came in to refuel and get more ammunition so they could go up again, and we were under fire the whole time.

Then, everything got quiet. The helicopters came in. The last of the flares died down. The generators started up, and we had lights at the camp again. But compared to what we'd had before, the base seemed dark and awfully quiet.

After a while Antonio and Snake came to the post where a few of us stood at the firing holes behind our sandbags.

"Are they gone?" I asked.

"For now," Snake said.

"What was that all about?" Irish asked.

"There were about 25 people inside the camp. In physical combat uniforms. They wanted to keep you guys penned down here, so you couldn't put the helicopters up." He grinned. "I think you're going to find lots of new ventilation holes in your tents."

There was a moment of stunned silence. We knew some people had gotten into the camp. But twenty-five? That was shocking.

"How did they get in?" somebody asked.

"They came through the village and cut a big hole in the fence. You know, those houses and buildings that are right up against the fence? We're going to have to clear those buildings out. That's why the guards didn't see them coming in."

"We can't do much until it gets light," Antonio said. "So take turns getting some sleep. We've set guards along the fence. They won't get past us again."

"Anybody hit?" Scott asked.

Antonio shook his head. "As far as I know, none of our people. The corps workers went inside the trenches under their buildings as soon as the shooting started. They seem to be okay too."

"We killed some of them though," Snake said. "And we took a prisoner. He'd been shot. He was disabled to the point that he couldn't continue to fight but didn't have time to kill himself."

"Kill himself?" I asked, shocked. The Peruvians didn't commit suicide.

"When we shook him down, we found a cyanide capsule on him."

"Was he a Peruvian?"

"Doesn't look it. We don't know yet. But we're assuming he was a zapper."

That left us speechless. Zappers are super James Bond types. They've already decided they are going to die. They come into a camp shooting, killing, blowing up things, doing as much damage as they can do. A Super Zapper could take on and kill 30 people. They are really good. Their attitude is that if they're killed, they're killed. They've already made their peace with the grim reaper. That was definitely not Peruvian. It was like something out of the Middle East or Vietnam.

The tents we lived in had bunk beds, but nobody slept on the top bed because it was above the sand bag wall. It was a good thing because Antonio was right. We had several new ventilation holes in the top of the tent. In fact, we could see daylight through some of them.

THE NEXT MORNING dawned soft and pretty—as if nothing had happened. A pink haze lay over the dark, verdant hills to the east; and the river beside our camp murmured as it moved by at a gentle pace. The smell of gun smoke still hung in the air though, reminding us of the events of the night before.

As soon as it was light, the helicopters went up to search the area and make sure the enemy had left. It's also very easy to see bent grass trails, sometimes even blood trails from the air.

When we were pretty sure the enemy was no longer around, we went out to search for bodies and weapons. Pretty Boy, Flash, and I were searching the area along the back fence when Flash stopped and pointed at the ground.

"Now this is interesting," he said.

The markings on the ground were unmistakable. A body had been dragged there. The Peruvians didn't drag their wounded or dead off. They carried them off.

A few minutes later we found the body with a hay hook in it and were speechless for a moment. That's what the Vietnamese used to do—put hay hooks into those who were wounded or killed and drag them off the battlefield so their enemies would not know how many people had been killed. Hay hooks were not Peruvian.

"Hey, Josh, doesn't this guy look a little familiar?" Flash asked.

It was the smallest of the three men we'd seen in Benchley's Bar just a week before, the guy who appeared to be Italian or French.

Then it dawned on me. "This guy is Vietnamese. They've got a bunch of Vietnamese over here training their troops."

"You think the Brit was one of them too?" Flash asked.

"Has to be." It was difficult to believe that someone from England would be in Peru training terrorists, but there was no other explanation.

When we searched the body, we found a state-of-the-art walkie-talkie inside his vest. We'd never found radios of any kind before, much less such good quality equipment, much better than what the US military had.

Later I was searching along the beach when I saw an FAL—a Belgium-made rifle—lying beside a bush. It was probably one of the most accurate and devastating weapons ever made for combat—far better than the American AR 14's, 15's, or 16's because it used 30 caliber ammunition like a machine gun and would penetrate light body armor at 300 meters. It was a single shot, three-shot burst, and was fully automatic. We'd never found a weapon of that caliber before.

But one of the guardians found something even more telling on one of the bodies—a map of the base, indicating where the helicopters were, where the ammunition was stored, where tents were, and where the corps of workers stayed.

The battle we'd just fought was a probing battle—a testing battle. The enemy had set up a complete perimeter and probed the camp.

AFTER THE DEA established the base at Santa Lucia, buildings had sprung up next to the fence overnight. That morning the DEA paid the people for their houses and buildings and bulldozed them so we could clear the area around the camp.

To beef up the defenses at the base, we started sending out night patrols, headed by guardians.

The man the guardians had captured turned out to be an Israeli mercenary. He had been on a leave of absence from the military. His country was furious when they found out he was in Peru fighting the DEA.

Obviously the Narco Traffickers were paying a tremendous amount of money to not only Vietnamese mercenaries but also British and Israeli mercenaries to come to the country and turn their soldiers into a fighting force.

We figured we had been doing some damage. It was okay as long as we were only finding a few pozos and a few drug lairs and destroying them. But when we began methodically catching hundreds and thousands of kilos of cocaine that was being processed, when we captured aircraft with Colombians aboard and confiscated them, we were hurting the drug traffickers; so they had joined up with the *Sendero* and were retaliating. That's why they'd hired mercenaries—to make sure they got rid of the gringos, to make us an ineffectual force.

But we kept right on doing what we'd been hired to do. Drug intervention.

The intel from Los Palmos was that there was still troop movement around our camps, and these troops were bribing the people with food, money, and alcohol to keep their movements quiet.

One morning Irish and I were getting ready to go out on a raid when Flash came in the tent looking upset. "Did you hear what the Peruvian Policemen are doing now? They're wearing civilian clothes under their uniforms."

"Civilian clothes?" I said. "In this heat?"

"Yeah, that way if we're attacked, they can pull off their uniforms and pretend to be workers. And they're sleeping in their clothes."

Irish just shook his head and smiled. "They've done that before. They're always getting nervous about something. Don't pay any attention to them."

"There's something else. Their officers seem to be trying to figure out ways to get out of camp. Their colonels and majors have already left—said they needed a vacation. So the captains and lieutenants are in command, and they're trying to get away too. They think something is going to happen."

"Just because they think it's going to happen," Irish said, "doesn't mean it will."

"The guardians are finding packages of food, money, and sets of civilian clothes under the beds in the barracks of the police and the workers. They're ready to desert at a moment's notice."

Irish laughed. "It's an old story. We've had times like this before. Probably will again. Don't worry about it. It will go away in a few days."

I wasn't convinced, because I'd noticed something else. When we went on missions, the Peruvian National Police were supposed to be making the arrests along with the DEA agents. Except most of the time now, there were several DEA agents and only one or two Peruvians. It became almost entirely a DEA operation.

"We won't let them steal. That's one reason they're not going with us," Polecat told me. Then he looked thoughtful. "But it seems like more than that is going on."

And even the people like Irish who had been in the program for years, admitted that the atmosphere at camp was thick with tension, like electricity in the air before a storm.

ONE FRIDAY, SINCE it was getting close to the weekend, it was possible we might have an attack even though the moon wasn't full. It wouldn't be full for another week. But it was dry. So it was possible that there might be an attack.

We sat around the tent after dinner and watched a video and played checkers. Irish and Scott and a few of the other guys started playing poker. Because I was an inspector, I needed to do some paperwork. I slipped a 9-millimeter pistol in the belt holster I carried in the back of my shirt along with two extra clips and walked the half mile to my shop at the back of the base, near the end of the runway.

When I finished the paperwork, I turned off the lights and immediately heard people moving, whispering.

I stepped out and walked to the side of the building and found the enemy moving in front of me, behind me, and beside me. They had sneaked onto the base—hundreds of them.

They were already past the claymores. The base was under attack. No shots had been fired, but we were under attack.

My heart pounded and my mind raced.

What do I do? Do I holler that we have intruders and get myself killed? Or do I try to run through this crowd as fast as I can to the tent where all the Americans are to give them the news?

Chapter Thirty

The clackers for the claymores were located in a small, protected dugout near the back of my shop. Although the *Sendero* had already passed the mines, the explosions would alert the rest of the camp. I slipped around the exterior of the shed, then crawled to the dugout and hunkered down in the dark and let my eyes adjust so I could see clearly. I tried to be as quiet as possible.

A partial moon revealed movement about 50 yards in front of my position—parallel to a long drainage ditch 4-5 feet deep. The ditch was designed to take rainwater to the river and made a perfect trench for troop movement. They were positioning themselves inside the ditch to turn it into a firing pit.

I was ready to set off the claymores, but at that moment something happened.

One of the Peruvian guards on the tower in that corner must have heard something. Normally the searchlights pointed outwards. He turned the light around to shine into the camp itself. Suddenly, all kinds of automatic weapons went off, shooting it out. The fight had begun.

I'd come to the battle basically unarmed. I had a pistol with three clips. One clip was in the pistol—a Browning high-powered 9 millimeter. In the first clip I carried dead man bullets or glazers. They were filled with little glass balls and a oil solution.

I'd decided I would only use them in a life and death situation because if I shot the enemy anywhere, in the arm, leg, or hand, and unless the wounded limb is amputated almost immediately, that person is going to die. It might take him 2 or 3 days, but those little glass balls are fractured inside and cut the interior of the body apart.

This qualified as a life and death situation.

The other two clips contained regular hardball, nine-millimeter shells. I'd gotten into a habit of not fully loading the clips because if they were fully loaded, the spring would compress and the weapon would misfire. So they only contained twelve bullets each instead of the usual fifteen.

So I had 36 bullets plus one additional bullet in the chamber of the pistol.

I had 37 bullets with which to go to war.

I crawled out of the dugout, slipped over to the back of the shop, and quietly pulled part of the chain-link fence off the side of the shed so I could get back inside and look for anything I might use as a weapon.

An entrenching tool—an army shovel—one with a head that falls down and locks—leaned against a post just inside the shed. Someone had sharpened it and left it there. I dropped the head forward at a ninety-degree angle and locked it in place.

A couple of shop rags lay by the trashcan. I also found a lighter with a long stem on it, used to light charcoal, and a can of MEK, a very volatile cleaning agent. Until just a few days before, we'd had plenty of bottles on hand for Molotov cocktails, but for some reason someone had come by to collect them. The MEK can was ¾'s full. I could stick a rag in it, light it, and throw the can. As soon as the flames got to the fumes, it would explode like a bomb and create a very hot, a very intense fire, just like gasoline, only hotter because of the volatile chemicals inside.

So my weapons were a huge Molotov cocktail, a shovel, and a pistol with a few bullets.

I formulated a plan.

As soon as the battle really got underway, when the chaos going on around me would mask my actions, I'd light the Molotov cocktail and throw it in the ditch where the enemy had set up firing positions.

I crawled out the back of the shed, bringing the shovel and the Molotov cocktail and lighter with me. Then I lay on the ground, hiding, watching people move past, mainly on the road in front of my shop. Intent on what was happening around the tents, they weren't looking for a gringo on the ground behind them.

The battle had started as soon as they'd shot out the searchlight. Soon the explosions of hundreds of pistols, rifles, and machine guns filled the air. The *Sendero* and Narco Traffickers seemed to have a large number of automatic guns. Typically when they'd attacked they'd used 12 gauge shotguns. But they were using new weapons: automatic weapons, rocket propelled grenades, and hand grenades. They were doing battle and doing it well.

The Americans at the barricades around the tents were the only ones firing shotguns—automatic 12 gauge shotguns that had more than the normal number of shells because they had an extension on them.

Strangely, the 30-caliber machine gun in the tower off to my left stopped firing.

We should have had about a hundred Peruvians helping to defend the base, plus the guardians, plus the mechanics, plus the pilots, plus some of the clerical workers who were all trained on weaponry. Yet I could only see returning gunfire coming from a few places, and those places were almost surrounded.

I knew the moment I did something, I was going to expose myself. But if I did nothing, I'd be discovered.

The adrenalin started kicking in—everything slowed down—like in slow motion. When that happens, your senses become very acute. You can see everything. You can hear everything. In a fight you can see them when they get ready to move a hand and get out of the way.

A couple of lines from *Sergeant York,* an old movie from the 40's, came to mind. "If you're going to shoot into a flock of geese, don't shoot the first one. Shoot the last one and then work your way up, and you can get the entire flock." Since I was behind the enemy, I was in a perfect position to take out the men at the back of the flock.

Then there was a line from *Outlaw Josey Wells.* "If you know you're going to die, get mad, get really mad. Fight as hard as you know how to fight, 'cause you're going to die, so you might as well fight as hard as you can fight."

And another line—from my grandfather. "You never give up. If you try to do something, you try to complete what you're doing. You never give up."

All that time I was lying on the ground waiting for the right time to act. Soon the decision was made for me.

Someone stepped over the dugout where we had the clackers and was right behind me.

He pointed his weapon down. I turned over, looking straight up a gun barrel.

I kicked him as hard as I could in the knee with my left leg and did a leg sweep with my right. He fell down.

Fortunately, his weapon didn't go off or he didn't have a shell, because he should have been able to kill me at that point.

I jumped on top of him and he started to fight. I hit him with the entrenching tool several times—almost taking his head off when I hit him in the throat with it. I could feel the man's pulses jerking under me, until he was still.

I'd killed my first man and killed him in hand-to-hand combat. And now I had another weapon—his weapon—a Chinese AK 47 with four clips. Gathering my small arsenal, I crouched down and returned to the front of my shop. Somehow I had to try to break through their lines and disrupt them so the people down at headquarters would have a chance.

I was facing south. The trench they were firing from ran east and west and began about 15 feet ahead of me to my left. I stuffed the rag into the MEK can, lit it, and threw the can as hard as I could. It fell smack dab in the ditch and blew up. Men screamed and flames shot up into the air.

Then I ran to the right, to the far side of the road, in line with the tents where the other ex-pats were posted, hoping to eventually work my way down to them. But there were too many people ahead of me. They must have thought a mortar had landed in the ditch because they didn't turn around; they kept intent on advancing straight ahead, just like soldiers are supposed to do.

I took out my pistol. It's not a very effective weapon but has less of a muzzle flash than the AK. Since they were just a short distance away, I decided to try to use the old trick—start shooting them from behind to see if I could get some of those people down before the pistol ran out of ammunition. I tried to count the bullets, but it's amazing how difficult it is to count the bullets when you pull the trigger more than one time.

It took three bullets to the head or chest to get some people down. With one shot they continued to fight. Within a minute or so I'd gone through all 37 bullets. I threw that pistol on the ground and took the AK and ran forward.

I thought about crawling, but if you crawl, somebody's going to spot you. You're moving too slowly. So I jumped up and ran behind a group of the enemy to my right and picked targets in the long trench to my left.

From that vantage point, I started picking people out by the light of the flares that were going off, by the light of the moon, and by their muzzle flashes. Because they were firing full automatic weapons, every fifth bullet was a tracer.

Lots of people when they're using automatic weapons only know one way to use them. Pull the trigger, shoot the entire clip, and put in another clip. I was shooting one bullet at a time. The AK is an excellent weapon, with a large caliber shell that can knock a person down.

My firing was slow, methodical. Every time I saw a muzzle flash in the trench, I fired at it.

At that point they must have realized someone behind them was trying to shoot them, because here came a hand grenade, rolling in my direction.

Automatically, instead of trying to jump down and protect myself from it, I grabbed it as soon as it hit the ground and threw it back. It was an old Russian style grenade with a handle, similar to what the Germans used in World War II—easy to grab and throw back. And just about the time it got back, it blew up. Fortunately it was over them and not over me.

I was doing things I'd never dreamed I could do. Like it was instinct. *Be mean*, I kept telling himself. *Be as mean as you possibly can.*

Some of the *Sendero* and Narco Traffickers were still moving around. Some were crouching or lying on the ground firing. Some were leaving the trench at the other end and moving along the eastern side of the camp. About that time the machine guns in the two towers on the eastern side began to fire again.

As I kept moving forward toward the tents, another man noticed me, a man with a large machete. I raised the rifle, and he knocked it out of my hand. So I grabbed the shovel. When he swung again, I swung back.

I caught him across the back of the hand, and he dropped the machete. Once again I knocked a man down with a leg sweep. Once again I jumped on top of him and killed him.

My plan to work my way along the fence on the west side, which led up behind the tents, wasn't working. Too many people filled that area. Instead I ran to my left and forward, taking out those ahead of me as I came.

When I got to within 50 feet of the sandbag walls surrounding the tents, I could see our guys firing. I found a little revetment with sand bags around it. The only thing I had now was the entrenching tool. I'd fired every bullet I possessed.

The tents stood only 50 feet away; but when I tried to get my legs under me, they turned to jelly. My whole body seemed to be shutting down. I figured the adrenalin must have burned every bit of sugar out of me. That had happened to me before but usually after the emergency. This emergency was just lasting too long.

"Help!" I screamed. "I need help!"

Chapter Thirty-One

SCOTT AND A couple of other guys poked their heads over the sandbags.

"Scott," I screamed, "I need help."

"Stay there," Scott yelled back, "we'll come out and get you."

Tracers bullets were coming in from every direction. Bullets thudded against the sand bags and ricocheted all around. The *Sendero* were aiming all their firepower at anything around the tents.

About that time Flash, Pretty Boy, and a bunch of other guys set their rifles on automatic or semi-automatic and put down a blistering firefight in my direction.

The Reverend and Scott ran out with their automatic shotguns blazing, clearing the way. They came out that 50 feet, and Scott grabbed me by the arms and pulled me over the sandbags. Then the Reverend grabbed me on the other side, and they dragged me to the tents, with the other guys shooting right over our heads to provide covering fire.

They got me behind the sandbag wall, and the first thing I saw was Rambo on all fours hyperventilating. Rambo was the new man who had strutted around camp, bragging about how tough he was. This was the first real battle he'd been a part of, and he couldn't take it.

They took me directly to the command tent and laid me on the floor.

"My God," Scott said. "You're covered with blood. You're shot to death."

Donnie was our medic that night, and he came back to the corner where I was, carrying an IV ready to go. "I'd better see just how bad you're hurt."

As far as I knew, I was just weak. But I might have picked up some bullets and not known it. I'd heard of that happening. People being shot and not knowing until the shock wore off.

But when Donnie examined me, he only found cuts and scratches—really deep scratches on my face and neck where somebody had clawed the thunder out of me.

"You're not in bad shape at all," Donnie said.

"I'm just so tired I can't move"

Donnie handed me a chocolate bar and a canteen.

I took a long drink, and stuck the entire chocolate bar in my mouth and started chewing it up as quickly as I could. Then I drank as much water as I could because my mouth was so dry. Within minutes the strength came back into my arms and legs.

They brought Rambo to the tent too, still hyperventilating; and Donnie gave him a paper bag to breath into.

As I lay there on the floor, I heard Blevins, our communications man, on the radio trying to call Lima, Peru. When we came under attack, we were to notify the Marine Corps guard. The marines were supposed to be monitoring a radio 24/7, but nobody answered.

"We're under attack," Blevins said, over and over again. "This is not a drill. We need help"

Nobody answered.

If help was going to come, it would be several hours away, but we needed to get the message to Lima.

Finally, somebody in the room said, "Call Atlas."

Atlas was on a different frequency on the radio. Atlas is located out in Colorado in a deep place under a mountain and was originally built as a bomb shelter for nuclear weapons. It was through Atlas that we communicated with our families back home.

Blevins called them. "We can't raise Lima. We're under attack and are taking incoming fire. We're fighting for our very existence. We have wounded. We have dead. Please call them on the land line"

So Atlas called from Colorado to Peru and finally got somebody to tell the marines to get on the radio. That took almost 20 minutes.

"We're under attack," Blevins told them. "Hundreds of people are attacking from outside the camp, and hundreds are inside the camp. We need help."

Meanwhile, the DEA and the ex-pats were fighting as hard as they could fight.

Our base commander had taken a month's vacation. The man sent in to replace him was in his seventies. He was a genteel, old man with a southern accent and a white mane of hair. But he was also a tough, old man, who'd served as an officer in Vietnam.

He came walking in with several of the guardians surrounding him, giving orders, telling everybody exactly what to do.

I heard several, "Yes, sir's" from the guardians. They treated him with great respect and their respect was not easily won. If the *Sendero* and Narco Traffickers had planned the attack to coincide with the base commander's absence in the hope that the base would be weaker because of it, they had made a big mistake.

"What was the problem with those machine guns in the towers?" he asked.

"Jammed," Antonio said. "The Peruvians put them back together wrong when they cleaned them."

"You got them working again?"

"Yes, sir."

"If the enemy hasn't disabled the helicopters, we need to get them up. Now!"

Feeling strong by then, I went with the guardians to gather the mechanics and pilots for a charge to the helicopters. We loaded our weapons with as many shot gun shells as we could. We loaded our pistols.

At my bunk I got my .357 Magnum and my speed loaders. I was fond of that Magnum and had hot blows in those particular loaders. They'll knock anything down. I got the FAL rifle and loaded up with every clip I had, but I couldn't find my shotgun.

"Where's my shotgun?"

"Scott's got it," Pretty Boy said. "That's the gun he used to come and get you."

So the pilots put on their helmets and picked up their pistols and rifles and decided to make a run for the helicopters and get them started. Of course, the mechanics were there, some of the DEA were there, and some of the guardians were there to provide a human shield around them.

We stepped out from behind the sandbag wall and started a massive automatic firefight and plowed our way through the enemy, guns blazing. First we made a 50-foot dash to the little revetment where I'd hidden earlier. Then we ran another 150 feet to the first helicopter revetment.

The revetments were open on one end with sandbags on the other three sides.

Surprisingly, the helicopters weren't damaged. Almost every night, in case an attack came, we loaded them with machine guns. We loaded them with fuel. But they would need more ammunition. So far no one had blown our ammunition up or shot it up, causing an explosion.

The DEA, guardians, and mechanics got down inside the revetments, firing at anything that moved, and there were a lot of people moving, a lot of people firing at us. As soon as the pilots got the helicopters started, and they were able to get five of them started, the enemy decided to come in mass—not just one at a time.

"Let's get these choppers up!" Antonio yelled. "Do it with guns blazing on both sides."

The Peruvian gunners hadn't shown up, so the mechanics were to help provide covering fire. Just as the helicopter hovered out, we climbed the revetments and jumped on board.

I went in the first helicopter. I was proud of that helicopter, proud of all my helicopters, but especially that one. I'd rebuilt it not once but twice.

Irish was the other gunner. A couple of DEA agents were already on board. Immediately we shot everything we had out the door.

First the helicopter made a tight circle around the interior of the camp.

"Keep your heads low," Polecat told everybody over the radio, "we're coming around our buildings and tents."

Then he let out a Texas cry. "Yee haw!"

And some of the other pilots were yelling too, just like they'd yelled in Vietnam when they were in their twenties.

Then we went around again and again, making ever widening circles, shooting everything we could.

I couldn't see the people below, but I could see muzzle flashes. Anything that flashed, I fired at, because it meant someone was shooting up at me. Bullets thudded against the skin of the helicopter, but as long as they didn't hit anything critical like the rotors or the transmission, the helicopter was going to stay up.

We cleared the area, but within ten minutes, I was getting low on ammunition and so was Irish.

"We've got to come in for more bullets," Polecat told the people below. "Get it ready for us."

As soon as we touched down, I hopped off.

Raol and Jesus and a couple of the other Peruvians came running up, looking frantic.

"We couldn't get at the ammunition. The door's padlocked. We don't have a key."

Irish and I ran back with them to the bunker where we stored our ammunition. I grabbed the rifle out of Raol's hands and started banging on the padlock with the gun. When the bar holding it loosened, I used the barrel of the gun to pry the lock off the door.

Then the crates of ammunition inside were either nailed shut or sealed with screws. So we started breaking into the boxes and prying them open. Others ran up to help and grabbed up cans of ammunition and took them back to the helicopter and put them in. But what should have taken two minutes took six or eight.

When we got the guns loaded up, Jesus and Raol got on as gunners; and the helicopter hovered back out because it still had plenty of fuel.

As soon as the next helicopter came in, we reloaded it. No one got out. We had a chain set up and were bringing ammunition to the revetment as quickly as we could, until we had all five helicopters rearmed.

Then I took up a defensive position behind the sandbags with the guardians.

By that time it was getting quiet. Just about the only shots we heard were coming from the machine guns in the helicopters, laying down covering fire. Occasionally an enemy gun fired, but there were no more bullets coming in the direction of the revetment.

It got quiet. It got eerie quiet.

Chapter Thirty-Two

SOON THE HELICOPTERS came back around. Now we had time to load them up correctly—to put the night vision equipment inside—and refuel. Then they went back up, to provide overhead fire.

The Reverend and I stood together watching the fifth one take to the sky.

He glanced over at me and smiled grimly. "Thank God we had the helicopters. I hate to think what would have happened tonight if we hadn't had them."

The helicopters kept going around and around. Any time the gunners or DEA saw any kind of ground fire, they shot their machine guns and rifles. Then the muzzle flashes would stop. Either the person on the ground had thrown down his guns and run, or he was dead.

Antonio finally told three of the pilots to come in, that we'd just keep two helicopters up the rest of the night.

Snake had a grin his face could barely hold. "Hey, Lazarus," he said, "we did it." He hit me across the back, and then hit Antonio as well, almost knocking him over. "Hey, Bond. We did it!"

Antonio smiled, the first time I remember seeing him smile.

When the first helicopter sat down, Polecat turned off the engine and let out a loud, "Yee haw!"

The crew peeled out and for a while we were all dancing around hugging each other like we'd just won the Super Bowl.

"Okay, you jokers," Antonio yelled at us. "We're not out of the woods yet. Get back to your posts."

We started back toward the tents.

"Not you, Henry," he was yelling at Snake. It turned out Snake's real name was Henry. "We've got to find out what happened to our Peruvian police. See if any of them are still around."

Snake grinned. "Whatever you say, Bond."

I followed the rest of the crew to our fortified positions, to the bunkers around our tents and stood at my post for a couple of hours, until one of the guardians told us, "Stand down. But stay awake. Don't go to sleep or anything."

The base was very peaceful then. I sat down on the ground. I had my rifle. I had my pistol. I was ready for action. All I did was lean up against one of the sand bags. The next thing I knew Scott was shaking me. "Hey, you better wake up."

I sat up and blinked. It was getting light out. "Was I asleep?"

Scott sat down across from me and laughed.

"We've been listening to you for a couple of hours," Raol said. He was standing guard at a gun port. "How can you sleep, Man? Don't you know we just fought a battle?"

"We were just getting ready to make Raol the new colonel of the Peruvian troops," Irish said. He was on sitting on the ground, leaning against the sandbags smoking a cigarette. "And Jesus will be his aide-de-camp."

"Hey, no way," Raol said, "I don't want that job."

"The brave Peruvian colonel and his major were hiding under their building with about sixty of their men. And guess what they were wearing when Antonio found them. I'll give you a hint. They didn't have their uniforms on."

I laughed. "Were they wearing dresses?"

"Hey," Raol said, "don't insult the womans."

"They had on civilian shirts so they could blend in with the workers. They're very brave, right, Raol? Like El Torro, the bull."

"Like El Porro, the chicken."

As the sky got lighter, a couple of things were very evident. We had a lot of dead and wounded, and there were lots of bad guys dead and wounded out in front of us.

"All right," Antonio told them, "as we move out. I want you to kick every person out there and make sure they're dead. If they have any kind of life in them whatsoever, shoot them a second time or a third time. We don't want them shooting us. And we don't have time to question them. Unless the person appears to be an officer. Then bring him to us. We have to question him."

So the first duty of the day was to shoot everybody a second time or a third time, until we got all the way out to our wall.

We had radioed for help. The embassy accused us of being offensive instead of defensive. That was so ridiculous it was almost funny. We'd been attacked by hundreds of *Sendero* and Narco Traffickers, who had come on our base with the intention of exterminating us. We'd had to fight for all we were worth.

The pilots had been spectacular. They'd never flinched.

The ex-pats, the DEA, some of the office support, and about 25 of the Peruvian Police had fought hard. But it was something of a miracle that we'd survived.

Now we needed help. The wounded needed to be evacuated. We needed more ammunition, more medical supplies, more warriors. The ambassador said the C123's in Lima could not come out to the area because it was not secure.

Our white-haired base commander looked grim when he called some of us into the operations tent.

"The intel from Los Palmos," he said, " is that there will be another attack tonight. The enemy is already getting ready for it.

"Now the ambassador doesn't want any one coming to our aid. He doesn't want to risk loosing any of his big aircraft. I think he has the idea that we're expendable. But Big Bill and Tomahawk are defying him. They're coming out anyway. And Big Bill is coming in Patches."

Some of the men cheered.

We all knew who those pilots were. They were two of the last surviving Air American pilots left over from the Vietnam War. Most of the C123 pilots had been shot down and killed. These men had lived and breathed adventure all their lives.

And everybody knew that Patches was a good luck plane, left over from Vietnam. No one had been killed aboard that plane, though it had been shot up so many times it looked like a patchwork quilt.

"They're on their way to Maza Mari to pick up ammunition and weapons. They'll be on the ground here for less than a minute. They're bringing some reinforcements too. Some more DEA and government agents. We've got to get everything ready. So you men," he gestured at a few of the men on my side of the tent. Be ready to help unload the planes the minute they land. You," he gestured at a few more men, "Get the wounded ready and put them on board. The rest of you will put down covering fire."

Big Bill was one of the few pilots who could do a full-blown combat assault to an airport. That means he could do a 360 degree dive at the airport, land at almost take-off speed, even under gunfire, lower the back ramp, off-load equipment, load the wounded on board, and take off again without ever shutting the engines down. The whole process only took 30 or 40 seconds on the ground.

"The ambassador told the pilots they could not fly the planes. He said, 'You can't take them into a combat zone.' Big Bill said, 'Bullshit, we're gonna go protect our people.'"

Everybody cheered and laughed at that, because Big Bill had to be angry to talk like that. He never used that kind of language.

When Big Bill radioed that they were coming in, the men on the ground were ready and waiting.

He did the 360. He touched down almost at take-off speed, came down the runway, and the cargo door came around. He did a 180-degree turn at the end of the runway.

The men inside had all the ammunition on rollers, and they came out the back. Off came the ammunition. We put the injured and wounded on board. The door came up as Big Bill was taxiing down the runway, and he took off. Then Tomahawk in the next C123 came in with more ammunition from Maza Mora. The back of the plane came down and a bunch of men came storming off, loaded to the hilt.

Then we had more weapons, rifles, ammunition, food, and more important medical equipment—more than what Donnie had over in his little building because it had been badly damaged during the battle.

At that point we loaded up any additional people who needed to go out, Rambo among them. The plane took off in the same fashion as Patches had—after 35 to 40 seconds maximum time on the ground, then climbed out, and headed back to Lima where the people could get some help.

It was strange to watch Rambo get on the plane to leave—a young guy, probably in his early 30's who had bragged about how tough he was. I'd seen a lot of men come and go since I'd been in Peru—other mini Rambos.

One morning we woke up to find a *Sendero* flag standing on the island in the river just across from our base. A couple of the new guys decided they were going to retrieve that flag, even though they'd been told not to. The battle flag had been purposely left there to draw the attention of the Americans.

They'd been told they were never to pick up things like that up. Never go out there and make a target of yourself.

But one of those guys flew over the island and while somebody held the other one by his fraidy belt, he reached down and plucked up the flag and came back to the base waving it. Fortunately nothing happened to them while they were retrieving it, but the flag could have been a booby trap. Those two guys didn't last long either.

And once when I had first come to Peru, I went on a mission in support of the DEA in *Sendero* country. We'd flown out to a small village in a Casa—a Spanish-built aircraft with two turbo-prop engines and their garrets. When this plane is in the sky, it looks like a flying box. The pilot and co-pilot had only been in Peru for thirty days, but they, like Rambo, also maintained macho images.

On board were some DEA agents as well as Peruvian workers who had come to chop down some small coca plants. One of the maintenance crews had asked to come along as well because they wanted to go out and see what it was like in the jungle. Fred was a member of that crew.

He was a crusty old man who reminded me of some of the weathered farmers I'd seen in Texas, with wrinkled, skin and gaunt faces. Fred loved to tell about the narrow escapes he'd encountered in Vietnam, about his miraculous valor under fire.

Just a few minutes after everyone but the pilot and co-pilot had exited the plane and set out to destroy the coca, bullets started ringing across the area.

All of a sudden an engine started on the Casa. Then the second engine started. The DEA pilots pulled up the rear tailgate and down the runway they went and flew out, without picking up any of the ground personnel there that day.

Fred went bonkers. He started yelling and running around making a target of himself while everybody else formed a fighting perimeter. Finally we got Fred to lie low too. One of the DEA agents saw people up on a hill shooting down at us and started returning fire.

The battle was over almost instantaneously because within three or four minutes villagers came out, while we were still crouched down behind any cover we could find, to sell us pop and ice cream. They had a better handle on when the battle was over that we did.

Boxer, one of the DEA agents, immediately got on the radio. "Where is our transportation? Where is the DEA Casa?"

It seemed the Casa had headed back to Lima. The pilots said they'd had to protect their aircraft; but at the same time they had deserted the men on the ground, left us there with no protection, no transportation. Those particular pilots were more interested in protecting their aircraft than protecting their people.

So there we were—a hundred kilometers from our primary base—in bad boy country with people trying to sell us ice cream and soda pop.

Finally a flight of helicopters came out to bring us back in.

A week or so later Boxer, Fred, and I were back in Lima at Benchley's when who should arrive but the two DEA pilots who had been flying the Casa.

Boxer leaped up from the table and accosted them before they could sit down, with Fred and me right behind him.

"What were you idiots thinking! You took off and left us out there to be skinned alive by the *Sendero*."

The pilot who resembled Buddy Hacket, except taller, took off his sunglasses and looked down at the three of us as if we were insects. Meanwhile his co-pilot who usually wore a smile, peeked over his shoulder. "Look, we're sorry about that. It was our responsibility to protect the plane. We were told to get out if any hostilities occurred."

"Didn't they also tell you to get your people on board before getting out?"

"We had to leave to protect the plane."

"What about protecting the people?" Boxer just glared at them for a moment. "Don't you ever, ever do anything like that again!" He turned on his heel and went back to his table because differences of opinion were not allowed at Benchley's, and the bar had become very quiet.

Later that same evening Fred had a few too many drinks and decided he was going to go talk to those DEA pilots and give them a piece of his mind.

"Come on, Fred." I patted his arm. "Just calm down. There is no need to say anything else to those pilots."

"They left us behind." Fred staggered to his feet, and Boxer and I grabbed hold of him and took him outside and put him in a taxicab.

Fred was still protesting. "Those bastards left us behind."

"We're all right," I told him. "Were you killed? Were you hurt?"

"No."

"We're not going to have a fight in public."

A few days later the ambassador called us in and told us the pilots said they had been under heavy gunfire when the Casa pulled out. But Boxer and I set him straight.

The ambassador shook his head and sighed. "These particular pilots have only been in the country for thirty days, but they've created more problems than all of you have created in the last couple of years." He sent those men out of the country too.

These were the images that flashed through my mind as I watched Rambo board the plane that day. He'd hardly said a word to anyone or looked anyone in the eye since the battle. I sympathized with him and thought that I myself might have been on all fours hyperventilating if I'd been younger and greener. Only caught out there at my shop like I was, I wouldn't have survived. It was a miracle I'd survived anyway.

And I probably wouldn't have survived if I hadn't been shot and stabbed and left for dead by the *Sendero* when I was working for the oil company. If I hadn't been attacked on the streets of Lima and determined that I was not going to be a victim again. If I hadn't had a grandfather who drilled into me, "Never give up. Never quit."

Later that day I was patching one of the helicopters when Antonio came up and just stood there, until I got to a stopping place.

"That was tough for you last night. Caught out there like you were." Antonio just looked at me soberly for a moment. "But you did all right."

"Thanks." I didn't know what to say. I was a little embarrassed. "You had your doubts about me, didn't you? When I first came on board."

Antonio looked down at the ground for a moment, shook his head. "You just--you seemed like too nice a guy for this kind of work. Too soft maybe. Too idealistic." He gripped my right shoulder. "But you did okay." Then giving me a quick pat on the shoulder, he turned and walked away. It was one of the highest compliments I had ever received.

But the battle wasn't over. Because the *Sendero* planned to return.

Chapter Thirty-Three

FINALLY, THE AMBASSADOR called over the radio. "You did a good job. You defended, which was legal." Probably some of the wounded who'd been transported to Lima had gotten through to him.

The problem was that the *Sendero* and Narco Traffickers were coming back for a second attack. About six hundred men had attacked us the night before. We had killed maybe a fourth of that force. We'd found about a hundred bodies on the base itself and in the perimeter of the base, but we had no idea how many bodies had been carried off. However, the *Sendero* and Narco Traffickers were bringing in more soldiers too. According to the intel from Los Palmos, their plan was to come back with more numbers, with more power than before, to finish what they'd started.

Even with the new ammunition and several new men, we didn't think we could survive another attack. For one thing the bad boys just might have a different plan of action. All the *Sendero* really had to do was get to the helicopters and disable them. Maybe they wanted to confiscate the helicopters. Maybe they thought the crews wouldn't possibly be able to get to them.

But why hadn't they taken over all the guard towers on base by shooting up through the floors? They had taken over two of those towers, but four had escaped capture.

And maybe there was a lot of truth to what Snake had said. The *Sendero* and the Narco Traffickers used the coca on a regular basis. Their foreign leaders might have been able to keep them from drinking, but they wouldn't have been able to keep them away from the coca leaves.

While the coca would increase energy and supposedly increase their mental alertness, it also causes anxiety, fear and paranoia and can eventually lead to insanity and death. Maybe that gave them the edge when they attacked villages of innocent people but blunted their edge when it came to major battles.

But if they had taken over the towers and managed to disable the helicopters, they would have eventually won—just because of their shear numbers. As the specialist had said, the base at Santa Lucia was not defensible.

Some of the Peruvian Military Police like Raol and Jesus had fought long and hard. Some of them died fighting, like four Peruvians who were manning one of the guard towers. But most of the Peruvian Military had hid during the fight, so we didn't expect much help from that quarter.

"Tonight," the DEA told us, "we're not going to sit here like ducks at a carnival waiting to be picked off. We're going to go find them before they get to the base. When we do, we'll let them start the war in the jungle—not on our base."

That was a big no-no. That could be considered being offensive. It was very much like the early days of Vietnam, when the American soldiers could not return fire until they had a dead or wounded soldier on the ground. They couldn't even unlock or load their weapons and defend themselves. That philosophy was back in place because some of the same policy makers were in place who had made the rules decades before.

So there we were. Out in the middle of nowhere. Not badly hurt, I was to stay at Santa Lucia until relief came in two days—at the normal shift change. But in two days we could all be dead. So we got busy preparing for battle.

We paid the civilian workers to fill sand bags for a nickel a sand bag. We dug out our bag of nickels and rebuilt the entire fortification in one afternoon, using great big plastic bags with fiber-glass inside them that weighed about a hundred pounds. For every 20 sand bags the workers filled, they got a dollar. A dollar was real money to those people.

Since we couldn't depend on the Peruvian policemen, we did our own guard duty that night.

The message came in just as the sun sank and darkness overtook the base.

"They're coming in now," Antonio told us. "They've been recruiting all day, so we're facing as many of them tonight as we faced last night. They're trucking them in, and they are about two and a half or three miles away. We're going out to meet them."

We sent out a helicopter fully NVG equipped with a chase helicopter behind it to start looking for the enemy. They weren't hard to spot. Some of them came in on foot and some of them rode in the backs of pickups and farm trucks—a huge convoy. They hadn't even bothered to turn off the headlights on their trucks.

They all started firing at the helicopter, so the DEA launched all six helicopters and returned fire. Doing big circles. Disabling some of the trucks, catching some of them on fire, shooting at anyone who shot at them until they had effectively stopped the convoy and prevented the *Sendero* from returning to Santa Lucia.

THE NEXT MORNING since no one had come to claim the bodies at Santa Lucia, we dug a big hole and used the bulldozer to put bodies into it and cover them up, otherwise they'd start to stink and spread disease throughout the camp. In the outer perimeters, we found more dead and did the same thing with them.

After the second battle, when we supposedly became offensive because we had prevented the *Sendero* and Narco Traffickers from returning, we got a big reprimand. All the pilots but one were ordered out of the country within the next week. They were fired. So Polecat, Erick, and Pretty Boy were fired.

All the DEA agents that had been aboard the aircraft were ordered out of the country because they had been offensive instead of defensive. That reduced our maximum strength way down. New people were coming in within a couple of weeks, but during that period we didn't fly our helicopters. We didn't go out on any interdictions.

The official version of the first battle was that it was a two-hour firefight with no casualties. But, the Peruvian colonel who had hidden under his building and changed into civilian clothes got a metal from the president of Peru for his gallant defense of Santa Lucia. But he hadn't fought. He hadn't fired a shot. He had hidden like a big fraidy cat.

One of the people we'd killed looked like a Yankee. We dug through his information and found out he had a British passport. Through Interpol we learned that he was a sergeant major in the equivalent of the commandos, which is like the SF for Great Briton. He'd retired and become a mercenary. He'd been one of the trainers, but he was not the man Flash and I had seen at Benchley's Bar in Lima. So we knew even before we heard from Los Palmos that there were other British mercenaries involved.

THAT WEEKEND I went to Lima for two well-deserved weeks off and found out that Toni, my maid, was going to get married, even though she was in her late 20's or 30's. A typical Peruvian man will not marry a woman much older than her late teens or early 20's. Rich or poor, pretty or ugly, women that age never got married. But Toni was going to get married.

So I decided we might as well make it a big party of it.

I made a deal with the priest to give her a formal wedding and paid a seamstress to make a dress. I hired a photographer to take pictures. I bought food and beer and invited everyone to a big reception afterwards.

But when the party was over and Toni had left on her honeymoon, the apartment was terribly quiet, terribly empty.

Shoppers and revelers filled the streets because the Christmas season was fast approaching.

Peruvians know how to celebrate Christmas, with all kinds of activities, but the hustle and bustle of shoppers, the parties, the decorations depressed me. I called my ex-wife and talked to my son forever. Terry had apparently made a complete recovery. He and his mother were getting ready to go to California for a big Christmas with Deborah's sister and parents.

I had no reason to stay in Lima, so when they asked for people to spend two weeks at Santa Lucia over the holidays, I volunteered.

Christmas at the base was supposed to be a quiet period of time. I would perform some maintenance on the helicopters and make a few flights. Except for a contingent of 90 policemen, a couple of cooks, and a few workers, all the Peruvians were going home. One other mechanic would be staying, Irish, the man who liked his bottle. As long as Irish didn't have access to a bottle, he was a fantastic mechanic. So the Americans would consist of two mechanics, two pilots, two DEA agents, and two guardians—eight in all. Flash and Snake were among those men.

The people in Lima said they'd send Christmas dinner out to us.

We only took the normal provisions with us. It was supposed to be a time of rest and relaxation.

It was anything but that.

Part Nine:
Merry Christmas

Chapter Thirty-Four

My first day back at Santa Lucia, I'd just left the Operations Tent when something very unusual happened. The owner of Los Palmos came driving up alone in a jeep.

Los Palmos was the world's biggest palm plantation, and John Reeves, the owner, had originally come from the United States. One of his brothers had built a large cattle ranch in Argentina. Another had built a palm plantation in Brazil.

Not only did their businesses prosper, but they also prospered the areas they went to, because instead of tithing 10% of their income, they gave 90%. They put small stores and businesses in the surrounding villages. They built schools and hospitals.

When the civil war started in Peru, the owner vowed he would not be driven away. He built a runway at the plantation to get his coconut and other produce to market and bought Electras, four-engine aircraft, to haul materials.

His plantation covered more than 100 sections of land and was well guarded with mercenaries from around the world. They even had 50 caliber machine guns and were better equipped than the stores to sell pop, corn, bread, *etc.* to the locals.

The people who worked at Los Palmos were employed for life—kind of like the medieval system. The owner was the king. He had a big satellite receiver and a complete communications center. All the small stores gave him intelligence reports. If anyone attacked one of his people, he retaliated like the Israelis do.

"If you kill one of my people," John warned the bad boys, "I'll kill 10 of yours." And he did.

The *Sendero* did not even try to attack Los Palmos.

Once a group of Colombian Narco Traffickers tried to take them on. They planned to assassinate the owner of Los Palmos, but they were all captured and executed. Then people at Los Palmos found out exactly who had paid those people to attack. They cut off the heads of the Colombians, packed them in dry ice, and put them in cardboard boxes. The boxes were loaded on shipping pallets, flown to Colombia, and delivered to the head of the Narco Traffickers with a message: "Don't do it again, or we'll come and take your heads."

Los Palmos didn't have any more trouble with the Colombians.

Their intelligence was very good, and they usually radioed when there was about to be an attack on the base at Santa Lucia.

But the people from the plantation never drove up to our base alone, and it was especially unusual for John Reeves himself to do so. Before when he'd come to the camp, he'd had a small group of guards with him.

He drove through the gate and stopped in front of the Operations Tent beside me.

"I need to talk to the camp commander."

"The commander is gone for the holidays. Do you want to talk to one of the guardians?"

Mr. Reeves squinted his eyes against the sun and glanced around. The camp looked especially empty at that moment, because no one but the tower guards and the guards at the gate were in sight. In just one week we'd celebrate Christmas, and everybody had left the day before.

"How many Americans are here now?"

"Eight—a couple of pilots, a couple of guardians—."

"I guess I'd better talk to all of you then."

He went in the Operations Tent while I rounded everyone up.

When we were all present and seated, Mr. Reeves leaned against a desk and took his hat off. He was medium height with thinning gray hair and a small muscular frame. He looked worried.

"I thought I'd better come over here because we've had some important communications I need to pass on to you."

"Why didn't you radio?" one of the DEA agents asked.

"Because they listen in on the radio. I wanted to deliver this message to you quietly." He took a folded handkerchief from his pocket and patted his forehead with it then put it back. "We've gotten word that the *Sendero*, the Narco Traffickers, and part of the La Drones are banding together because they've noticed the workers and Peruvian military leaving. They are pretty upset because they've been driven away from this base every time they try to attack. They're upset because of all the dead they left behind on their last visit. So they are going to attack right after Christmas before everybody gets back."

It got so quiet in that tent that we could hear the radio playing in the Peruvian officers' quarters.

"How many of them?" I asked.

"The talk is that they're going to get several hundred people together for a surprise attack. They are going to try to overrun the base and kill or capture all the Americans.

"They want the helicopters, so they are not going to burn them. The Narco Traffickers are going to pay big money for them and use them to build their own air force."

"Where would they get the pilots?" Flash asked.

"I don't know. But they probably have pilots lined up."

That was possible. They had the money to buy just about anything they wanted.

"They believe they have a good chance of capturing the base now because they know you have very few people here. I'd take this threat very seriously if I were you."

As soon as he left, we called Lima on a security link and told the people there what Mr. Reeves had told us.

"We have no such information," the guy at the radio told us. "Let me ask around."

He was gone from the radio for a few minutes before coming back. "We don't think this is really going to happen."

"Can we speak to some of the ex-pats?"

"Just about everybody is out on vacation. We don't really have anybody here. By the way, we're going to send a special flight out with your Christmas dinner—a special flight on Christmas Eve. Turkey, dressing, pecan pie, pumpkin pie. Just keep a low profile. Don't take this rumor seriously."

When the conversation ended, we just looked at each other. There wasn't a person in the group who was not taking the warning seriously.

"Do you think we should tell the Peruvian police about this?" Flash asked.

"What Peruvian police?" Snake spoke up.

I had a sinking feeling in the pit of my stomach. "Aren't they here? Ninety of the Peruvian police are supposed to be here."

Snake grinned. "'Supposed to be' yeah, but most of them left last night. They all piled on boats and busses and went to their villages. And some of them took off for Lima a couple of days ago. I visited the barracks about an hour ago and only found a few people—a few guards and a couple of cooks—maybe 15 people in all."

It took a while for the shock of his words to sink in.

Irish closed his eyes and shook his head. "If the *Sendero* make a serious attack, we don't have a prayer, do we?"

Flash got to his feet. "Then maybe we'd better keep this to ourselves until we find out what's going on. Don't say anything to the Peruvian Police. By the way, did anyone get breakfast this morning? All I saw was coffee. When I asked the cook, he said all the food was gone. Maybe we'd better check."

"Okay," Snake said. "Let's do a recognizance of the kitchen and the personnel, see exactly where we stand and meet back here in an hour."

In the kitchen Flash and I discovered that virtually all the food was gone. We went to the commissary where the frozen food and canned goods were stored, and the shelves there were almost empty too. We did find coffee and some tea bags, but no soft drinks of any kind.

"What happened to the food?" I asked one of the cooks—a man with a big belly and a bowl haircut.

"It was like this when I come in. Somebody clean out everything. The police. The workers. They all take it home for their families."

"What are we supposed to eat?" Flash asked, looking angry.

"Can you buy us some things at the local market?" I asked.

"I see what I can find. But nobody have a lot of food now. It's Christmas in a few days." He flashed us a toothy grin.

So about the only thing we had to eat were our Meals-Ready-to-Eat (MRE's)—pre-packaged meals that contain meat, crackers, beans—enough food that a person can survive, but not exactly what we wanted to eat for breakfast, lunch, and dinner.

When we met back in the Operations Tent, we discovered that not only were almost all the Peruvian police gone, the Peruvian commander was gone. His assistant was gone.

The helicopters had been idle for a couple of days. We decided we'd better get them up. Maybe if we put them up on a regular basis, we could fool the *Sendero* into thinking we had a lot of people on the base, but there wasn't much we could do with only two pilots. Both the DEA agents were trained pilots, so they went up too so they could refresh their memories about how to fly. I could fly a helicopter, and so could Snake. The pilots took the two green helicopters up and flew over a *Sendero* camp; and when they came back, Snake and I went up in a gray and a green helicopter, with a guardian and one of the DEA agents at each door with their guns sticking out.

Raol and Jesus were in camp, and we knew we could trust them. So we started taking them up as well.

As it began to get dark, we told the Peruvian policemen to be sure and walk the perimeter of the camp. Every now and then we fired off flares and parachute flares, so we could see the area across the river and so the enemy would get the idea that there was a lot of activity at the camp.

A couple of nights we heard the enemy discussing us over the radio. "Maybe there are more people at Santa Lucia than we think there are. We know their helicopters are flying."

"No, they're just putting on a charade of some type," was the reply.

It sounded as if what Mr. Reeves had said was true. They were watching the camp. They were planning an attack. But it also sounded like they had spies inside the camp. Why else would it occur to them that the helicopters they were seeing were part of a charade?

We needed a better plan.

If the camp were attacked, the helicopters did not have the range to evacuate us to a safe location.

Flash and the other pilot pulled out some maps of the area and pointed out several hills that looked defendable.

The next day we flew over these hills and picked out three about fifteen to twenty miles apart and fairly flat on top with steep sides, hills we could use for runaway points if we were attacked. Then between our flights around the villages, we started filling up barrels of fuel and boxes of ammunition and MRE's and putting them aboard the helicopters.

We found some shovels and picks, and Flash, Irish, Raol, and I flew them out to the first hill and unloaded them. Then we filled sand bags and dug some trenches on top the hill to build fighting positions.

The idea was that if Santa Lucia were about to be overrun, we could desert to the hill, refuel the helicopters and set up a fighting camp.

The next day we went to the next hill and did the same thing, until we had all three hills set up. If the *Sendero* managed to access one hill, we'd desert to the next hill.

The third day Jesus met Flash and me at the landing pad when we came back after flying over the *Sendero* villages.

He looked nervous. "We got some more people." He nodded in the direction of five or six Peruvians who were standing outside their barracks, smoking cigarettes and talking. "Those are some of the workers and a couple of police that leave. They come back."

"What are they doing back?" I asked.

"They says they fight with they wives."

Flash laughed. "They all said that?"

"That's what two of them says."

"That doesn't sound likely."

Flash was suddenly sober. "Maybe they're part of the attack force. What do you think, Jesus?"

Jesus shrugged. "Juan comes with them. He is a good man. But this is big money. So is possible. I don't know."

While I was watching the group beside the barracks, they shot casual glances in our direction. Were they acting suspicious? Or was I just imagining it? But then if they weren't part of the attack force, why would they come back before Christmas?

That night we decided we definitely would not tell the Peruvians of our plan. If we had to leave the camp, we'd get on four of the helicopters and blast out of there. The only Peruvians we'd take were the two door gunners. We trusted them. We didn't trust anybody else.

We didn't want the Narco Traffickers to get the helicopters we left behind, so we rigged them with mines activated by remote control so we could blow them up in place if we had to desert the base.

Since we didn't trust the Peruvian police, every night we took turns walking patrol and shooting off flares. We tried to meet every ten minutes. If somebody didn't show up in ten minutes, we went looking for that person. Something might have happened. Maybe somebody was already inside the camp.

We carried portable radios so we could stay in communication but still wanted to have physical evidence that everyone was alive and well. We slept in shifts. Two hours of guard duty, two hours of sleep. Since there were so few people, we only got four hours of sleep a night. For the most part, we were eating MRE's.

But things were looking up. It was getting close Christmas Eve and the big Christmas dinner we'd been promised. Then we got a message: "The weather on this side of the mountains is bad. We'll try to send the food on Christmas Day."

But on Christmas morning there was another message: "The weather is still bad, so we're not coming."

Irish and I were sitting in the mess tent eating MRE's when one of the DEA agents passed through the tent and gave us the news.

We laughed.

"Yeah, we knew they wouldn't send anything," Irish yelled after him then turned to me. "Maybe the Peruvians will take pity on us and give us some chicken."

The Peruvians had been eating MRE's too, but some of them had managed to buy or steal some chickens. So they were going to have fried chicken for Christmas.

I remembered seeing a few cans in the cabinets. "I think there was some tuna in the kitchen."

Irish rolled his eyes. "Oh, yeah, that sounds really delicious."

"You'd be surprised what you can do with tuna. And maybe there are some other things in there. I'm going to take a look."

I like to cook, and Irish was curious. So he followed me to the kitchen. We searched the storerooms again and found several cans of tuna at the back of a shelf and some leftover chili and corn bread in the refrigerator. The MRE kits contained crackers I could crumble up.

Then I went to the village and bought some eggs to mix with the tuna and crackers then seasoned the whole mixture with mustard, garlic, and dried onions to make tuna patties. When they're fried, they taste like salmon.

I added water to the chili and a little hot sauce to turn it into a spicy treat.

One of the DEA's contributed a bottle of Irish whiskey. Flash laid some Cuban cigars on the table.

We stared at them in astonishment.

"Where did you get Cuban cigars?" I asked.

"I work for the embassy, don't I? So I order them from Cuba. They come right to my mailbox."

My mother always sent me the same care package for Christmas: fried apricot pies and pecans, roasted in butter, garlic, and salt.

So our Christmas dinner consisted of chili, tuna patties, apricot pies, pecans, Irish whiskey, coffee, tea, and Cuban cigars. Then that night at midnight we met to wish each other a Merry Christmas, as was the custom in Peru.

That was when Snake, who had been monitoring the radio all night, passed on the bad news that the *Sendero* and Narco Traffickers had not been fooled.

"A couple of them were talking about how we only have two pilots in camp. They said those two pilots are doing all the flying. The attack is still on for tomorrow night."

Flash looked angry. "They've got spies in the camp. How else could they know we only have two pilots?"

"Maybe it's because we're only sending up two helicopters at a time," I said. "When we go on missions, we usually send four helicopters. We've got six people who can fly helicopters, so let's take them up four at a time."

"What's the use?" Snake said with a sneer. "Flash is right. They've got spies in camp."

One of the DEA looked thoughtful. "I think it's worth a try. If we take four helicopters up, it will certainly prove that we have more than two pilots in camp."

"And let's make a little noise tomorrow morning," I said. "Wake them up in case they spend too much time celebrating tonight."

So the next morning we launched all four green helicopters and flew right over La Cheeza and shot off our guns just outside the village. There was a scurry of activity below and more than the usual number of bullets came in our direction.

That afternoon we launched four gray helicopters and flew over La Cheeza and a couple of other areas where we knew the terrorists would be coming from.

Snake met the helicopters when we came in that afternoon and was grinning broadly. "They bought it. This one guy says, 'There's not two helicopters flying, there's four of them. We saw green ones this morning and gray ones this afternoon. They were flying a mission.' This other guys says, 'Maybe the entire crew has been brought back inside the camp, and we didn't know it.' They bought it. They are calling off the attack."

But we were especially vigilant that night, just in case the bad boys changed their minds. We kept a couple of helicopters in the air off and on all night, scouting the area. We set off flares and walked the fences, but no one attacked or even came close to the camp as far as we could tell.

The next day we put up four helicopters again, and the *Sendero* and Narco Traffickers again reported that the DEA had resumed its missions. That meant they probably wouldn't attack. It also meant they were not getting intelligence from inside the camp.

We were relieved but remained vigilant.

When our 14-day period was over, the C123's arrived to take us back to Lima. All of a sudden here came a full compliment of Americans. The Peruvian workers and police arrived at the base by the truckload.

Those of us who'd occupied the base over Christmas break were a ragged crew—we'd had little sleep, not much food. But we'd managed to defend the base without firing a shot.

FOR THE NEXT six months we tracked down, killed, or arrested the foreign mercenaries. The last person we captured was an Israeli lieutenant colonel who was the head of the operation.

He had hired the Brits. He had hired the Israelis and even a few Vietnamese to come in and train the *Sendero* and Narco Traffickers. He had also taken a leave of absence from the Israeli army for a year to go to South America and make a bunch of money. The Israelis sentenced him to life in prison.

In the meantime the wanted posters with our pictures on them reappeared. Only now they stated that the $150,000 could be collected either in the jungle or in Lima. So all of a sudden we were at risk in the town where we were normally safe.

Two days later one of the people shown on the posters, a major in the Sinchis branch of the Peruvian army, was assassinated as he came out of his home to get in his car to drive to work. Five or six people shot him so many times he was like Swiss cheese. The poor guy never had a chance to pull his pistol out to defend himself. His son, daughter, and wife witnessed their father being killed on the front door step.

The next year, in 1992, Abimael Guzman, head of the *Sendero Luminoso*, was captured. The notebooks we had taken at the Colombian jungle lab, containing telephone numbers and addresses, had helped bring about his capture.

The Peruvians were very careful to keep Guzman alive so he wouldn't become a martyr.

As soon as we got rid of the leadership, the *Sendero* and Narco Traffickers went right back to their old tactics. They were no longer a fighting force. They would hit and run. Steal and murder. But were no longer an effective fighting force.

However, I was a marked man. I was told that I'd have to leave Peru.

"At least you *can* go back," the Reverend said when I told him I'd sold my restaurant and planned to go back to Texas. "I doubt that I'll ever see the states again."

"Why?"

"IRS. At the end of the Vietnam War I married a girl over there and stayed and worked for her father. So I didn't file any income tax forms. Then before the country fell, we moved to the Philippines. When she died, I went back to the states; and the IRS made my life miserable.

"They claimed I owed them millions of dollars in back taxes. You're supposed to be innocent until proven guilty but not as far as they're concerned. They garnished my wages and seized my bank account so I couldn't fight them. Then they harassed me at every turn. I was offered this job and took it in a heartbeat. We have a couple of other people on this base in the same situation."

The Reverend went on and on about how the IRS abused its power.

Chapter Thirty-Five

A FEW MONTHS later I was back in Texas. I stayed with my mother in Dallas for a while so I could spend time with Terry. He was in great shape. In fact, he was so busy with baseball practice and other activities that he hardly had time for me. So I moved my belongings to the farm my grandfather had once owned in East Texas. The farm I now owned. I'd saved some money while I was in Peru, so I set to work at once fixing the place up.

The house itself was in pretty bad shape. I probably should have leveled it, but I couldn't. Instead I hired a crew of men to help me remodel it.

Oddly enough one of those men was Michael Branagan—the kid I'd envied when I was a boy because his parents let him use bottles and cans as targets instead of sticks. He was a big man now, tan from working in the sun and with salt and pepper hair that was thin on top.

"Michael, I've got to know. Are you a good shot now?"

I was sitting on the front steps, and Michael had just carried some lumber up to the porch and laid it down. He stopped to wipe the sweat out of his eyes. It was just the first of June, but already the weather was hot and humid because it had rained the day before, filling the air with moisture and the scent of sweet, damp earth.

Michael eyed me suspiciously. "What do you want to know that for?"

"I just remember you being pretty good with your rifle when you were a kid. Are you good now?"

Michael grinned. "I thought you were going to call me out." He shook his head. "Put it this way. I'm just glad I can bag my meat at the grocery store. I bet you're still pretty good though, aren't you? Being in the line of work you were in."

"Yeah, it helped to be able to shoot straight."

Looking serious, Michael sat down beside me on the steps.

"I was following some of the stuff that was going on in South America. That's a vicious bunch down there." He squinted his eyes against the sun and stared out across the hills. "But weren't you kind of old for that kind of work?"

"Most of the guys I worked with were Vietnam vets. Oh, the DEA hired young men, but they were the ones who got killed." I thought about Underdog and Flash and the way they'd saved the lives of the men in the crashed helicopter. I thought about Polecat and the others who had been with me in the swamp for three days. And about the way Scott and the Reverend had rescued me during the Battle of Santa Lucia. "Don't let the gray hair fool you. Those old codgers in their 40's or 50's are some of the toughest men I've ever known."

"Ever have to kill anyone?"

Fortunately, the phone rang. "That's between me and God," I said as I got up.

I had to find the phone under some construction clutter inside the house. Deborah, Terry, and my mother were the only ones who had my number, so I figured my mother was calling. But she wasn't. The voice was familiar though. "Hey, partner, had enough time off?" Scott drawled.

I laughed. "Not likely. A few years probably won't be enough time. What are you up to?"

"Well, looks like I'm going on a treasure hunt."

"A treasure hunt? In Montana?"

"No, in Africa. I just signed on with the United Nations."

"I thought that was supposed to be a peaceful group. What do they want with you? And what do they have to do with a treasure hunt?"

"Seems the Israeli Secret Service lost some diamonds."

"The Mossad?"

"Yeah. They lost four hundred million dollars worth of raw diamonds that they were going to trade for arms. The guy who bought the diamonds was captured by the Russians and just happened to have a heart attack. Only he hid the diamonds before the Russians captured him. Now everybody's looking for them. We've got to find them before the Russians do."

Scott paused, but I knew what was coming.

The front door was standing open. I could hear birds singing, and I had a good view of the overgrown meadow that was my front yard and a tall stand of trees that covered the hill just beyond the meadow. Everything was kind of wild in its present state but plush and green. Ripe with promise. A man would have to be crazy to leave this Texan paradise and go to Africa on a wild goose chase.

"Interested?"

I guess I've always been a little crazy.

Printed in the United States
131675LV00004B/13/P